M000042424

The Name of Love

The Name of Love

Lowland Romance Book 4

Helen Susan Swift

Copyright (C) 2018 Helen Susan Swift
Layout design and Copyright (C) 2020 by Next Chapter
Published 2020 by Liaison – A Next Chapter Imprint
Cover art by Cover Mint
This book is a work of fiction. Names, characters, places, and incidents are the
product of the author's imagination or are used fictitiously. Any resemblance
to actual events, locales, or persons, living or dead, is purely coincidental.
All rights reserved. No part of this book may be reproduced or transmitted in
any form or by any means, electronic or mechanical, including photocopying,
recording, or by any information storage and retrieval system, without the
author's permission.

I dedicate this small book to you, the reader. I hope you find half as much pleasure in reading my words as I did in writing them.
Helen Susan Swift

'Read with joy and an open heart': HSS
'Reading brings us unknown friends': Honore de Balzac

Chapter One

I never liked my name. Mary Agnes Hepburn. The Hepburn part was acceptable, just, but *Mary;* plain old Mary followed by Agnes. *Agnes,* for goodness sake. I cannot think of an uglier name than Agnes. I used to ask my mother why she could not have chosen something a little different, something mysterious or romantic, but no, Mary Agnes it was and Mary Agnes it had to remain.

'Mary was the name of queens,' Mother told me, with a smug smile that did not help in the slightest.

'Well, the queens can keep it,' I said.

'So must you,' Mother's smile did not falter. And that was her final word on the matter.

It was many years before I became reconciled to my name and then only in the most unusual of circumstances. I will relate them by-and-by, but as in all tales, it is best to start at the beginning and finish at the end, so that is what I shall do. Now, bear with me, please, as I wend through this story, and I hope you will smile when I smiled, cry when I cried and feel all the emotions in between. Being Scottish as I am, I am not very good at showing my feelings, but when I do, nobody is in any doubt of what they are. Just stand clear when I unleash my temper, and all should be well.

Perhaps it was because of my plain Mary name, or maybe because of my black temper, but I was not the most popular of women. I had a tendency to remain apart from other people, which drove my parents to distraction. I was, and am, also stubborn, wilful and generally a *thrawn besom*, as we say in Scotland. I don't think there is an exact English translation, but a cantankerous troublemaker may be as close as you will get. In short, I am my own woman and always have been. You may see what I mean as I unravel the tale of my name and the sealed document that waited to spring its unpleasant ambush upon me.

One thing I did enjoy was to be outdoors where the cool rain could wash my face. I always preferred bird-song to the most beautiful choral music, and the singing of the wind to the most accomplished of formal orchestras.

'You'll never find a husband that way,' Father said when he came across me working in our walled garden that late autumn day of 1787. 'Leave that sort of thing to the servants.'

'I like it here,' I leaned on the handle of my fork. 'I like working with plants and animals.'

Father shook his head. 'What sort of man will want a wife with a sun-browned face and rough hands?'

'I'm not looking for a man,' I said, truthfully enough, for I had long given up the idea of romance. That sort of thing was for others, not for women such as me. Knights on white chargers ride to the rescue of beautiful princesses with fanciful names and long golden locks, not plain Marys with often-tangled red hair.

Father dismounted and whistled for the stable-boy to care for Hector, his horse. Father always gave his horses the name of Classical heroes, so he had Hector, Ajax and Achilles. Homer would have been proud of him. Personally, I always preferred the name and character of Ulysses to Hector. I like a man with brains as well as brawn. Perhaps that was one reason I could not find a man who would suit me. My male contemporaries were good men enough, dependable workers, honest as the day was long, but take them away from farming, and their minds would flounder like a coach in a peat bog.

'Now, Mary,' Father put his one arm around my shoulders. 'You must start to think about your future. Your mother and I won't be here forever, you know.'

'I know,' I said. 'In about twenty or thirty years I will worry about that.'

'You don't want to be an old maid,' Father said. 'You don't wish to live a lonely life.' He spoke quietly, as he had done so often before. Although I knew he meant to give kindly advice, I was not in the mood to listen. 'Your mother and I are perfectly willing to help find you a decent man. There are dozens who would leap at the chance of marriage with you.'

'Name one,' I said as my temper heated up. 'Name one decent man who would leap at the chance of marrying a sun-browned woman with rough hands. Name me one decent man who would leap at the chance of marrying me for myself; not a man who would marry me because in twenty or thirty years I will fall heir to your property.'

That was rather a long speech for me, for I was not prone to conversation.

Father smiled. I suppose that after twenty-odd years of marriage to my mother, a woman's temper did not bother him much. 'I will do better than name one, Mary. I will bring one to meet you. Then I will bring another and another until you meet a man with whom you feel comfortable.'

'Comfortable!' I allowed my temper to control me, rather than me controlling it. 'I don't want a man with whom I feel comfortable! I want a man who loves me.'

Father raised his eyebrows in that infuriating manner he had. 'I thought you were not looking for a man at all.'

'I'm not.' My temper calmed as quickly as it had arisen. I was not sure if Father had trapped me or if I had unwittingly revealed a truth I did not wish to have known.

'That's all right then,' Father kissed me on the forehead. 'You won't have any objections to your mother and me looking for you.' When he stepped back, tall, bronzed and kindly, I knew that I would never find a man like him. That was another part of my trouble, you see; I had a father who could do anything, and I had never met a man, young or old, who could match him in temperament or ability.

'You won't find a man for me,' I told him.

'Maybe we will and maybe we won't,' Father said, 'but if not, it won't be for want of trying.' His smile took ten years off his age. I could easily see why Mother had fallen for him all these years ago.

As I watched him stride into the house, whistling, I knew that life was going to become that little bit more complicated. When Father decided to do something, he put his whole heart into it, whatever *it* was. I sighed, remembering his efforts to improve the few hundred acres that we called our own. Not content to supervise the new drainage scheme, Father had to go down with pick-axe and shovel to lead the workers in the field. When we built new field boundaries, he was there, lifting and carrying the stones for the dry-stane dykes that now snake across our land. When he had new cottages for the tenants built, he helped draw up the plans and ensure every home had slate roofs and a decent vegetable garden; very impressive for a one-armed man. With that sort of example, is it any wonder that I like to spend my time out-of-doors rather than sitting quietly sewing, painting or playing the pianoforte like other unmarried women are supposed to do? I have only my father to blame for that, bless his interfering heart.

Perhaps it is because I am an only child without any brothers that Father treated me as much like a son as a daughter until he realised that girls should be brought up differently. By that time it was too late, the damage had been done and rather than sitting prettily, I liked to ride on horseback dig holes in the garden or walk in the muir. Is it any wonder that I could not find a man? Which man would want a woman as unconventional as I was?

Even knowing Father's unflagging energy, I was surprised just how quickly he began to round up the local bachelors and bring them to Cauldneb House, our less than romantically-named home. For those of you who can't translate guid Scots, *cauld* is what you may term as cold and a *neb* is our word for a nose, so we lived in Cold Nose House. It is hardly an evocative name, but once you have experienced one of our winters, or indeed one of our springs or autumns, you will understand the aptness of the description. The wind here howls straight from the north and east, cutting through layers of clothing like a knife of ice.

Unfortunately for romance, the neb in question is not the nose situated on a human face. Our neb is a protuberance on a range of high muirland or low hills, thrusting north-eastward toward the German Ocean. A muir, you understand, is what you may call a moor.

If you have read my account so far, you may wish to know where Cauldneb happens to be located. You will realise by now that we are in Scotland. Fine; so your first thought may be for the majestic Highlands with its tartan-bedecked clansmen with their Gaelic speech and great chiefs. We are not up there. Cauldneb is in the south of the country, a score of miles east of Edinburgh, on the northward slopes of the Lammermuir, exposed to winds from north, east and west. There are many good points; the views are splendid, over the plain of East Lothian, across the chopped blue bite of the Firth of Forth to the fertile fields of Fife. Our fields were equally as lush as those in Fife, which was another major factor in Cauldneb's favour. Oh, and the Firth of Forth is an inlet of the German Ocean, like a smiling mouth inviting trade into the heart of Lowland Scotland.

For good or bad, Cauldneb was home. King Malcolm II, the Destroyer, had granted the lands to the precursors of the Hepburn line back in 1018. Although there are other Hepburns in the area, we predated them by some centuries, owning Cauldneb without ever becoming ennobled or grasping for more. We were and are happy with our wee bit land; our blood and sweat had made it what it is, and generations of our ancestors lie in the local Kirkyard. Some, naturally, have ventured abroad.

Simon Hepburn rode to the Third Crusade from the ancient, crumbled keep that predated our house. Walter Hepburn fought with the Grey Wolves against English invaders in the 14th century. David Hepburn crossed to High Germany to fight the good fight for somebody or other in the Thirty Years War and my father, Andrew Hepburn had lost an arm experimenting with a new reaping machine.

And now there was me, plain Mary, the last of the line. Father's quest to find me a husband was not entirely from a desire to save me from lonely spinsterhood. He also had the interest of the family in mind. So did my mother.

'You see, Mary,' Mother said, 'there is only a limited time during which you can produce a baby. That is why women marry young. You are already twenty years old.'

Produce a baby. How cold-blooded that sounded. How practical. How unromantic. 'I know how old I am, Mother.'

'Well then, Mary, it's high time you thought of somebody else for a change.'

That was grossly unfair.

'Think of your poor father. He needs to know the family line is secure before he dies.'

Before he dies? Father is forty-five years old and as fit as Neil Gow's fiddle.

'You have to find a husband, Mary.'

Yes, Mother. So you keep telling me.

'So what are you going to do about it?'

That was how mother spoke. She ranted about her own thoughts and ideas and then demanded my answers to problems that only she believed existed.

'I believe that Father has it in hand, Mother.' I said, as much to keep the peace, or rather to get some peace, as anything else.

'Good.' Mother's mood altered as rapidly as a sparrowhawk catching its prey. *Was I the prey?* 'We'll soon have you all settled with a respectable man, Mary, don't you worry.'

'I was not worrying, Mother,' I assured her. That was no longer correct. I was beginning to worry now. I had no intention of being rushed into marriage with some dull-as-ditchwater supposedly-respectable man who was probably twice my age. Or with some brain-numbed clodhopper of a farmer whose imagination did not extend past the nearest midden heap. A midden heap is a dunghill, in case you were wondering.

I tried to push the thought of my parents' matchmaking out of my mind by helping Mr Mitchell the gardener. Middle-aged, with perennially dirty hands, he had an encyclopaedic knowledge of every plant in the garden. I enjoyed his company, which annoyed my mother, who pretended to care for me mixing with the servants even less than Father did.

'Don't get too familiar,' Mother said. 'The servants are not our friends.' She arrived in the walled garden when Mr Mitchell was explaining the elements of grafting. Mr Mitchell was making sure I understood each step before progressing to the next.

'Mitchell!' Mother often spoke sharply to the servants when she was trying to convince me of my elevated position. 'Cook needs more potatoes.'

'Yes, Mrs Hepburn.' Mr Mitchell said. 'I'll get them to her directly.'

Mother watched him stroll away. 'You'd better get washed, Mary. It is not a gentlewoman's place to get her hands dirty.'

'Maybe I'm not cut out to be a gentlewoman,' I said.

'Maybe not,' Mother was unperturbed. 'Be that as it may, you *are* a gentlewoman. None of us can escape our destiny.'

'I can try,' I said.

I knew that mother was correct. I was the last Hepburn of Cauldneb. It was my destiny to produce sufficient heirs to ensure the continuation of the family line.

'We are what we are born to be,' Mother told me. 'We have a guest coming a week this Saturday. Mr John Aitken.' Her smile wrapped around me like a snake. 'You'll like him.'

'Oh.' I could not think what to say. *John Aitken.* 'I don't know any Mr John Aitken. I thought I knew all the local gentlemen.'

'Mr Aitken has recently moved into the area from up north,' Mother's smile did not falter. She touched my shoulder. 'The family has purchased Tyneford. You don't know him, Mary. I know that you will like him.'

'Will I?' I looked away. 'I should choose my own man.'

'If you find somebody,' Mother said, 'let me know, and I'll judge his suitability.' She stepped toward the exit of the walled garden. 'I've already judged the suitability of John Aitken.'

'I might not like him,' I said.

'You will,' Mother told me. 'He is very respectable and eminently suitable.'

When Mother left, I felt as if she had closed the door on my life. I knew my mother. In her eyes, the match was done and dusted. It was only a matter of time before I walked down the aisle and became Mrs John Aitken, a respectable married woman to raise a whole brood of little Hepburn-Aitkens suitable to continue the family line for another seven hundred years. I knew that Father would try to persuade this John Aitken fellow to change his name to Hepburn.

The thought that Mother had already decided my future was not pleasant. I could not bear to remain where I was. I had to move, I had to walk. I had to feel the wind in my face and the ground under my feet.

With the name John Aitken rolling around inside my head, I nearly ran from our walled garden.

Nowadays everybody had heard of Lammermuir or Lammermoor as some people tend to spell it. Sir Walter Scott immortalised it in his novel *The Bride of Lammermoor,* which brought hundreds of readers to our neck of the woods. However, in my day nobody came to Lammermuir. The mail coach from London to Edinburgh passed at a distance, and the odd hardy traveller ventured onto the heights to cross to the villages of the Merse, the fertile, lowlands of the far south-east of Scotland. Apart from the farmers and shepherds and an occasional gaberunzie man - that's a wandering pedlar - very few people knew Lammermuir.

Let me explain. Lammermuir is a plateau of low heather-ridges on the south-east shoulder of the nation, bleak, empty and open to the grey sky above. I had grown up wandering the muir, so I knew it well. It was bare, wind-tortured and in winter desolate beyond description. I loved it. I loved the space. I loved the emptiness. I loved the wildlife, the wild hares and the lizards, the kestrels and sparrow hawks. I loved the plants peeking from the burns that gurgled through the heather. I liked the fact that I could be alone with my thoughts.

That afternoon, my thoughts were as dark as the peat holes that waited to trap the unwary. I was used to my life of freedom; now I knew that would change if my beloved mama married me off to some unknown stranger. *John Aitken: what an uninspiring name.*

To access Lammermuir, one has first to negotiate an initial steep slope that leads to what is essentially a plateau. I took the slope at speed, leaning my hands on my thighs to propel my legs through the heather. Ignoring the rasping of my breath, I pushed on, to reach the summit with my heart pounding.

Lammermuir stretched forever before me with a constant breeze stirring the heather, so it appeared like a browny-purple sea. As always, I stood there for a long minute to drink in the scenery and taste the Lammermuir wine. That is what I call the scent of this magical area, where the breeze carries the fresh smell of the heather, sometimes mingled with earthy peat or the wild aroma of sheep. The combination of space, heather and fresh air, all under a canopy of God's good heaven, makes Lammermuir a place like no other. It is my bit, as we say here.

When the hammering of my heart calmed down, I walked into the muir. I took long steps, revelling in the freedom, enjoying the play of light from the sky on the undulations of the landscape. I breathed deeply, trying to forget Mother's intention to marry me off to some unknown man. *John Aitken.* The name seemed as dull and featureless as one of the boulders that littered this muir. After half an hour of constant walking, I perched on a handy rock to think.

When I smelled the smoke, I knew that all was not as it should be. As there was no house in the area, there were only two possibilities; either some careless person had set the heather on fire, or somebody was operating a whisky distillery. Of the two, the latter was more likely. At that time there was open warfare between the illicit whisky distillers and the Excisemen the length and breadth of the country. The tax on small-scale distilling was so high that only a very few could afford it, leading to hundreds, if not thousands, of illegal distilleries springing up. Most were in the Highlands, but we had our share in the Lowlands as well. Naturally, the government were opposed to this tax evasion, and employed a small army of officials, often backed by regular soldiers, to quell the trade.

I knew that some of these illegal distillers could be a little bit rough, so you will forgive me being cautious as I approached the source of the smoke. Now, you may be wondering why I did not turn away completely from any source of danger. Well, if the truth is told, I am generally not an inquisitive sort of woman, but I do like to know what is happening, especially in my own muir. Lifting the hem of my skirt away from the longest of the heather stems, I slowly approached the smoke, watching for the ankle-trapping peat holes that wait for the unwary.

The distillery was so cleverly hidden that I could not see it. All I could see was the drift of smoke above the heather. If I had not known Lammermuir, I might have believed the smoke was mere mist. Going down on all fours, I crawled closer, feeling for an opening.

'Who the devil are you?' The voice was nearly as unfriendly as the hard hand that grabbed my shoulder and yanked me upright.

I looked around, squirming in the man's grasp. 'I am Mary Hepburn,' I said, more chagrined at having been caught than afraid. 'Who are you?'

The man was of middle height, with an unshaven face and red-rimmed eyes. He was not in the slightest bit handsome. 'Mary Hepburn, are you? What are you doing snooping around here, Mary Hepburn?'

'I live around here.' I twisted in his grasp, trying to escape. I may as well have tried to fly to the clouds. 'You, however, do not.'

'What do you have there, Peter?' A second man joined the first. Younger but every bit as unkempt, he held a stout cudgel in his hand.

'A woman, Simmy.' Peter shook me, much as Gibby, our terrier, would shake a rat. 'I found her snooping around.' His broken-toothed smile was unpleasant.

'A woman?' Simmy came closer, tapping the cudgel in his left hand. 'What shall we do with her?'

'I've got some ideas on that,' Peter leered closer. His grip tightened. 'We could teach her to mind her own business.'

'Aye,' Simmy tucked his cudgel under his arm. 'We could.' I would put him at 28 or 30, a stocky, broad-shouldered man. 'Let me have her, Peter. I'll show her things she won't forget.'

Peter smiled again. 'We can both show her things she won't forget.' He pulled me closer, shaking again. 'Mary Hepburn is it?'

'There's lots of Hepburn's around here,' Simmy said. 'Too many blasted Hepburns.'

'I know a quiet spot where we can deal with this Hepburn,' Peter said. 'Nobody will disturb us there.'

Until that point, I had not been seriously alarmed. Now I had a notion of what they intended. 'Take your hands off me!' I tried to shake myself free. 'Let me go!'

'She's got spirit, this one.' Peter dragged me across the heather, with Simmy at his side, laughing high-pitched. 'I like a woman with spirit.'

'Let me go!' I swung an open-handed slap at Peter, catching him across his mouth.

Rather than obeying my command, Peter shook me again. 'You'll pay for that you little minx. By God, you will!'

'Who'll pay for what?'

My muir seemed crowded that day. I looked up at the new voice. The owner was a gentleman by his voice and appearance; a tall, long-faced man with his hair tied back in a neat queue under a silver-embossed tricorne hat. He stood on a small clump of heather, legs apart and hands on his hips, yet it was his eyes that attracted my immediate attention. You can tell a lot from a man's eyes. This gentleman's eyes were deep brown, fringed by lashes that any young woman would have been proud to own. At that minute they were focussed on me.

That initial image will be with me always.

'We found this woman snooping around, Captain Ferintosh.' Peter's suddenly humble voice reinforced my belief that the newcomer was a man of importance.

Captain Ferintosh? This man was either a ship's captain or an officer in the army. *How romantic!*

'Did you indeed?' Captain Ferintosh stepped down from his heather. He tapped Peter's arm with the cane he carried. 'Release her.'

Peter obeyed at once.

'Do you have a name, my Lady of Lammermuir?'

'I have, Captain Ferintosh.' I dropped into a passable curtsey, given the circumstances. 'I am Mary Hepburn.' I said no more, for I did not think it altogether wise to release my address when rough men such as Peter and Simmy were within hearing. The less they knew of me, the better.

'Miss Mary Hepburn.' My gallant captain met my curtsey with an elegant bow. 'I am glad to make your acquaintance, Miss Hepburn, although I would wish that the circumstances and company were somewhat better.' His smile revealed even white teeth.

'I think your arrival was extremely fortuitous, sir,' I said.

'You two.' Captain Ferintosh snapped at Peter and Simmy. 'Leave us!'

Simmy and Peter stepped back at once. I swear that Peter looked nervous.

I did not expect what happened next. Captain Ferintosh swung his cane, catching Peter a sound stroke across the shoulders. As Peter gasped, Captain Ferintosh pushed him backwards onto the heather. Simmy dodged the captain's next blow, unbalanced and fell face forward onto the ground. At once, Captain Ferintosh stepped forward, flicked up the tails of Simmy's coat and landed a smarting blow across Simmy's posterior.

'That's what you deserve for maltreating a lady,' Captain Ferintosh said, adding another in the same place as Simmy yelped and tried to wriggle away.

I could not describe my feelings as my gallant captain dealt so decisively with my erstwhile attackers. Surprise, undoubtedly, but also a measure of satisfaction as Captain Ferintosh landed a third stroke across Simmy's tight breeches before turning his attention to Peter. The two rogues retreated across the muir at some speed, with Captain Ferintosh administering his own brand of justice to help them on their way.

'I am sorry you had to witness that,' Captain Ferintosh returned with his cane under his arm and his eyes alight. 'I was not the most edifying sight for a lady to see, and I can see that you are undoubtedly a lady of breeding.' His wink was as unexpected as his boyish grin. 'Although, Miss Hepburn, I must admit to some perverse pleasure in dealing so with such rogues.'

'I shared your feelings, sir,' I tried to keep the laughter from my voice. I am sure Captain Ferintosh read it in my eyes. 'Thank you for rescuing me, Captain Ferintosh. It was worth my few moments of anxiety to witness such an entertaining sequel.'

'The pleasure was entirely my own,' Captain Ferintosh said. 'It is not often that one comes across a damsel in distress, especially not such a beautiful damsel as you.'

'I am anything but beautiful, sir,' I denied his words while simultaneously savouring them. Compliments were not frequent in the Hepburn household.

'You are misinformed, Miss Hepburn,' Captain Ferintosh hesitated slightly. 'It is *Miss* Hepburn is it not? Or has some fortunate gentleman already captured your heart and you are a Mrs?'

'It is Miss Hepburn,' I said. 'There is no gentleman, fortunate or otherwise.'

'In that case,' Captain Ferintosh said, 'the gentlemen of East Lothian are sorely lacking in taste to allow such a charming lady as you to run free.' He bowed again.

'Their laxity is my good fortune, for if you had already been married; your husband would undoubtedly keep you secure in your boudoir, thus denying me the pleasure of your company.'

I stifled my smile and shook my head, quite enjoying this verbal exchange with such an eloquent gentleman. 'Sir, you have all the charm of a Frenchman, coupled with the boldness of a Crusading knight. The married lady's lack of freedom of which you speak persuades me not to seek a gentleman of my own.'

Captain Ferintosh's eyes sparkled as he heard my response. 'For shame, Miss Hepburn. You surely would not deny a gentleman your company for such a small matter.'

'Freedom is a noble thing, sir,' I tested the scholarship of this fascinating man.

'So said John Barbour,' Captain Ferintosh passed my little examination, proving himself to be more than a charming smile. 'Do you value your noble freedom, Lady Mary?'

I curtseyed in acknowledgement of this rapid promotion from Miss Hepburn to Lady Mary. 'I do, sir. I do like to walk abroad on the muir.'

Captain Ferintosh swished his cane. 'I am sure that an understanding husband would allow such freedoms,' he said. 'But he might advise you to carry a pistol.'

The suggestion was so unusual that for a moment I could not bring clever words to my mouth. 'Do women have such weapons, sir?'

Captain Ferintosh's smile vanished. 'If you were my lady, Miss Hepburn, I would ensure you carried such a weapon. I would not wish you to walk abroad in such a dangerous place as this stretch of moorland.' His eyes crinkled at the corner. 'However, I can only dream of having that gratification.'

I curtsied, not sure what to say although my mind was in a whirl. 'I have walked Lammermuir all my life, Captain, without danger until today.'

'There, then,' Captain Ferintosh said. 'I am being overly cautious for your safety.'

'I thank you for your concern, Captain.' I could not resist looking into his eyes. Those dark lashes were nearly feminine, yet he had already proved himself more than a match for two of the most disagreeable men I had ever met.

'Do you wish to continue your walk on the moor?' Captain Ferintosh did not use the local pronunciation. 'If you have no objections to my company I will happily accompany you wherever you wish to go.' He swished his cane. 'I can assure you that these two unpleasant gentlemen will not bother you when I am here.'

'I have no fears of my safety when I am in your company, Captain,' I said truthfully. I hesitated, torn between my desire to find out more about this man, and a realisation that it was growing late. Darkness fell early on the muir. I looked at Captain Ferintosh, wondering.

'You are asking yourself if you are safe with a strange man up here in the heather,' Captain Ferintosh may have read my mind.

'Am I safe?' I asked the direct question.

'Your *reputation* may not be safe,' Captain Ferintosh said gently. 'If you are seen with me, tongues may wag and inferences made.' He shook his head. 'We both know how minds work; people will see us together and make up stories to fuel their imaginations. Before we know where we are, what begins as a rumour will be accepted as a fact and there!' He swung his cane again. 'In the popular mind your reputation is in tatters, and no decent gentleman will be seen near you.' He smiled. 'The loss is entirely theirs.'

I laughed at his manner of speaking although I knew his observations were accurate. Or most of them. 'I am not sure if the gentlemen would rue the loss of my company.'

'Then more fool them,' Captain Ferintosh said. 'Any man who would not seek your company does not deserve the title of man.'

'You are too kind, sir.'

'You do not allow yourself sufficient credit, Miss Hepburn.' Captain Ferintosh said. 'Now, have you decided? Shall I escort you across the heather? Or have you had sufficient excitement for one day.'

I could not tell the captain that I wished more, much more, of his company. That would have been a most unladylike statement, however true. Instead, I sighed and looked upwards, where a wind dragged grey clouds across the sky like a servant drawing the curtains on the day.

'I fear I must return home,' I said.

'Then home is where you will return,' Captain Ferintosh bowed again. 'I shall escort you to a juncture that we both agree is safe.' His smile was as ready as ever. 'Do not fear, Miss Hepburn, 'I shall not allow anybody to see us together. Your reputation is as secure as your chastity.'

I did not say that at that moment I did not give a tinker's cuss for my reputation. Indeed, if people did begin to talk, then dull John Aitken would have no interest in me. I would be free to pursue my own pursuits... I looked sideways at Captain Ferintosh. Now I had a new quest, once I gathered my thoughts into some logical sequence.

'Thank you, Captain.' It felt strange to drop into a formal curtsey among knee-high heather, but everything about this meeting seemed queer. 'I live at Cauldneb, a few miles to the north on the fringe of the muir.'

Captain Ferintosh lifted his eyebrows as if in surprise. 'Cauldneb?' He shook his head. 'You must be Mr Andrew Hepburn's daughter.'

'I am all of that,' I agreed. 'Do you know my father, Captain? I feel sure he would have spoken of you.'

'I know *of* your father, Miss Hepburn. We have never met.'

'Then you must come home with me, Captain.' Suddenly I was wild to have my father meet this most interesting man. 'I will introduce you to each other. My father is the kindest man who ever lived, sir. You must like him. I will tell him that you saved me from these two...'

I stopped, not sure if a lady should use the words that rushed to my lips.

'These two?' Captain Hepburn was teasing me, I am sure. 'These two what, Miss Hepburn? These two scoundrels perhaps? Blackguards? Rogues? Sorners?'

'Pick any of these terms sir,' I did not confess that I had a somewhat sterner name in mind. I was suddenly glad I had not spoken it.

'I will pick scoundrel,' Captain Ferintosh said. 'It is a word that a lady can safely use. Even the daughter of Mr Andrew Hepburn of Cauldneb.'

'I will tell Father that you saved me from these two scoundrels.' I swung my arm, imitating the captain's movements with his cane.

Captain Ferintosh smiled. 'I am sure you would introduce me splendidly. However, I will leave you at the edge of your father's policies.'

'I would like to introduce you,' I said. 'You did save me.'

'Not today, Miss Hepburn.' Captain Ferintosh shook his head. 'I may meet your father some time.'

I could not shake that man. I rather liked his stubbornness. I did not want a man who would bend to my every whim. A man should be strong as well as kind.

What was I thinking? I had only met Captain Ferintosh once, in unique circumstances. He was not my man and never would be.

We parted company at a five-barred gate at the dry-stane dyke that marked the southern boundary of father's policies. Within the dyke, all was farmed and secure. Without was the heather of the muir. I hesitated on the border, unsure on which side of the dyke I belonged; was I a Muir-woman or was I settled and secure?

'Fare ye well,' Captain Ferintosh said.

I faced him, looking directly into those marvellous eyes. I wanted to say, 'until we meet again,' but that would have been tempting fate. Not sure what to say, I curtseyed.

'Thank you, Captain,' I managed at last.

He nodded, turned and walked away. I watched him stride up the slope into the muir, hoping he would turn. Not until he was little more than a speck did he do so, raised his hand in salute and disappeared.

Chapter Two

Only when I lay in bed did I realise that Simmy and Peter had immediately known Captain Ferintosh. That must mean the captain was famous in certain circles, if certainly not my own. I had not asked anything about the captain; I had not even asked which ship he commanded or which regiment he served in. Nor did I know why he happened to be on Lammermuir that day. There was so much about Captain Ferintosh that I did not know.

I hugged myself as I remembered his dark eyes and the manner in which his mouth curled as he smiled. I recalled my feelings of satisfaction as Captain Ferintosh's cane curled around Simmy's rump; I had not known that side of me. It stirred something dark I knew I must explore, albeit within the private corners of my mind. There were other feelings too, which will keep to myself. I resolved to find out more about the mysterious Captain Ferintosh, such as why he had been so reluctant to meet my father.

I knew the two of them would soon be the most amiable of companions, once I introduced them. I smiled as I thought of them discussing the latest developments in farming, or shooting pheasants or partridge in the fields. I had not asked Captain Ferintosh if he was a sportsman. I was sure he was; he had that rugged, outside look about him, yet without the heavy lumpishness that so many farmers have.

Life had opened a new door for me, one that exposed a bright, exciting room into which I fully intended to step. I sighed as Mother's mention of John Aitken returned to the forefront of my mind. No, I told myself. I was not interested in staid John Aitken. I had another, much more interesting man in my life now, a dark, mysterious, romantic man who had already demonstrated his chivalry. I smiled, pulled my pillow close and allowed myself the most delicious thoughts that I certainly will not share on the pages of this journal.

'Well, Mary,' Mother spoke across the width of the breakfast table next morning. Father did not speak. Father was alternately reading the newspaper and studying details of the court cases he would be dealing with today. I have not yet told you that my father was the local Justice of the Peace, dealing with the petty cases that crop up in every rural community.

'Well, Mother,' I was not sure what else to say.

'You are one day closer to meeting Mr John Aitken.' Mother never missed an opportunity to press her case. You will know the expression 'like a dog with a bone.' Mother was like that; if she had something in her mind she would speak about it endlessly until her victim; usually me or Father was too worn down by the constant verbal and emotional barrage to put up any more resistance.

'Yes, Mother.' I countered Mother's assault by passive agreement. While my words said one thing, my mind was elsewhere, wondering how I could learn more about Captain Ferintosh.

'Six cases,' Father mumbled, making notes on a pad with pen-and-ink. 'Some thief is stealing quality foodstuffs and clothing. I'll have to watch that.'

'Once you meet him,' Mother ignored Father's semi-coherent muttering, 'you won't wish to meet anybody else.'

'Yes, Mother,' I agreed, thinking about Captain Ferintosh's most amazing eyes.

'Poaching and trespass,' Father trimmed the nib of his pen with a pen-knife. 'Some bold rascal has stolen a coach from Inveresk.'

'You have similar tastes to this gentleman.' Mother continued. 'You can't say that about many young men, Mary. You are the most awkward child.'

We had been through this conversation before. 'I am not a child, Mother,' I said.

'Drunkenness,' Father added to his notes.

'No, Mary, you are not a child,' Mother said. 'I am glad you finally realise that. You are a nearly of age to become a woman. It's high time you began to accept your responsibilities. You must take an interest in things outside your own immediate concern.'

'Yes, Mother,' I remembered the speed with which Captain Ferintosh had acted and the manner in which those two scoundrels accepted his authority. I liked Captain Ferintosh's term: *scoundrels*. It sounded just right. I repeated it: *scoundrels*.

'Scoundrels,' Father said.

'Scoundrels, Father?' I interrupted Father's work. 'Who are these scoundrels?'

'My word, Mary.' Father looked up. 'You must have been listening to your mother's advice after all. You are taking an interest in things outside your immediate concern.'

I hid my surprise. I had thought that Father was too deep in his pending court cases to listen to anything that Mother prattled and here he was, aware of all that had been said. 'Yes, Father.'

'I have half a dozen cases today,' Father explained. 'Four of them are small affairs of only local interest, simple trespass, poaching and drunkenness. The other two are for smuggling illicit whisky, a pair of scoundrels who were caught sneaking into Haddington with puncheons of raw peat reek.'

Peat reek, you may wish to know, was our name for illicitly distilled whisky. 'Whatever happened to innocent until proven guilty, father?' I wondered if the whisky smugglers were the same two scoundrels I had encountered on the muir.

Father looked up. 'These two were caught with the puncheons draped over the back of a pony. There is no doubt as to their guilt.'

'What will happen to them?'

For a moment, Father looked concerned. 'I can sentence them to jail, fine them or order them to a higher court. I won't decide until I hear all the evidence.'

That was better; Father had not decided on the gallows' noose just yet.

'These two are only petty criminals,' Father said. 'They might be young men led astray by the supposed glamour of smuggling, or family men who need some extra money to feed their families. If so I will be lenient. If I find they have a history of smuggling and law-breaking; if they are criminals by habit and reputation, then I will have to be stern.' He shook his head. 'I don't like sentencing men or women to long periods of imprisonment or worse.'

I could not see Father as a hanging judge. 'Worse?'

'I could sentence them to the stocks, the pillory, or even a whipping.' Father looked decidedly sorrowful. 'No, Mary, my position as a magistrate is one of terrible responsibility. I do not take my decisions lightly.' He looked away. 'If only I could catch the people at the top of the tree, the kings and queens rather than the pawns. Then I could end the whole thing.'

I thought of a king of crime, imagining a Jonathan Wilde, Johnny Armstrong or Rob Roy MacGregor. There was undoubtedly an aura of romance about such men, despite, or perhaps because of, their lawless activities. Men of spirit seemed so much more interesting than the dull-but-worthy farmers who tilled the soil and took no risks year after year. 'Is there such a person as a king of crime?'

Father put down his papers. 'Not as such,' he said. 'Perhaps in Edinburgh or London or some such place some people organise thieves to rob specific places, but out here the worst we have to contend with are the sorners, gypsies and whisky smugglers.' He sighed. 'They are bad enough in all conscience.'

I have already spoken of the whisky smugglers, and we still have roving bands of gypsies, although not as many or as troublesome as they were back in my youth. Sorners are virtually unknown now. They were men and women outside the law who wandered from place to place causing trouble. Often moving in bands a dozen or a score strong they had been known to terrorise small villages or even take over lonely farm steadings. I had never seen a sorner and never wished to.

'If there were such a person as a king of crime,' I wondered, 'what would you do?'

'Your father would do whatever he thought best.' Mother could not stand listening to a conversation without putting in her tuppence worth. 'He would call out the army and hang the rogue.'

'After a fair trial,' I said.

'There would be no need for a trial for such a man,' Mother could be much bloodier than Father. If she were to be the local magistrate rather than Father, there would be no crime in the area, for the simple reason that she would have any culprit hanged even before he could plead guilty.

'Surely that would be very autocratic,' I said.

'This country needs a strong hand,' Mother said. 'We are far too lenient with the ragamuffins that infest the highways and byways.'

When I thought of the two distillers who had attacked me, I could not suppress my shudder. *Thank goodness for Captain Ferintosh.* 'Maybe you are right.'

Mother had not missed my reaction. That woman had eyes like a cat. 'That's not like you, Mary,' she said. 'You're normally more indulgent with law-breakers. What's changed?'

'Oh, nothing.' If I mentioned the scoundrels, I would also have to talk about the captain. I was not yet ready to do that. I wished to hug his memory to me for some time yet. Captain Ferintosh was mine and mine alone.

My attention wandered away from my mother's conversation. *John Aitken indeed.* I scoffed at the name. I had no need of a John Aitken, a name as plain as Mary Hepburn. I had Captain Ferintosh, a braw gallant, as the song goes, a man of style and authority, a man to whom excitement clung like mist to the heather. I imagined Captain Ferintosh on the quarterdeck of a fast smuggling lugger, or Captain Ferintosh in command of a King's ship, giving orders to defeat the French, or

Captain Ferintosh in the brave scarlet of the Army, marching in front of a scarlet-coated company in some bloody European battlefield.

'You're not normally so bloody,' Mother caught my thoughts as she interrupted my dreaming.

'I've been listening to Father,' I said. 'He's quite right, you know, Mother. Some of these rogues are the most unpleasant of men.'

Mother nodded, slowly. 'I am glad that you finally realise what an important job your father does.' I knew that she was wondering why I had changed my mind. The memory of Simmy and Peter was fresh. Only Captain Ferintosh could chase away the horror of that brief encounter. I hugged his image to my breast, wishing I had time to pursue my dreams. I could not do it here, at the breakfast table.

'I will spend the morning within the walled garden,' I said.

I felt mother's gaze on me. 'Think about Mr John Aitken,' she said.

I had no intention of thinking of John Aitken. I had a far more interesting gentleman to occupy my thoughts.

Chapter Three

I did not see him until I had been working for quite some time. I looked up from the apple tree I had been pruning, and there he was.

'Captain Ferintosh!' I did not try to hide my pleasure. 'How did you get in?'

'Miss Hepburn.' Captain Ferintosh stepped clear of the shadows. 'I apologise for disturbing you in this manner.'

'Oh, no,' I brushed the hair clear of my eyes. My hair always had a tendency to flop across my eyes, especially at the most awkward moments. 'There is no need to apologise, Captain Ferintosh.' I waited to see what he wanted.

'I've been watching you all day,' Captain Ferintosh swept off his tricorne hat and made an elegant bow.

'Oh?' I curtseyed as best I could. 'Why is that, pray?'

'There is only one reason for a man to spend five hours watching a young lady,' Captain Ferintosh said.

'And what may that be?' I raised my eyebrows, wishing that I was more presentable for the good Captain. I wondered what he had seen of me. What had I been doing that morning? Nothing embarrassing I hoped. I had been helping Mr Mitchell; that was perhaps not ladylike, but it was harmless.

'To admire everything she does,' Captain Ferintosh said.

I gestured to the garden. 'I was not doing anything special,' I said.

'Everything you do is special to me.' My gallant Captain stepped closer, replacing his hat.

'Why, thank you, sir.' Once again I was enchanted by those dark eyes with the long lashes.

'I crave two favours of you,' Captain Ferintosh said. 'I know I have no right to ask.'

'Ask anything,' I said, recklessly.

'The first is the opportunity to see you again.'

'That I will grant, gladly,' I said with a smile, as my heart beat faster. I was sure that Captain Ferintosh could see my agitation. 'If it can be arranged.'

'I am aware of the rules of decorum,' Captain Ferintosh said. 'I will not compromise your respectability by having you being seen with me unchaperoned in a public place.'

'It would be more scandalous to be caught in a *private* place with a strange man.' I said, wishing I had a fan to open and hide behind. Captain Ferintosh must have seen the flaming blush that crossed my face.

'Am I so strange?' Captain Ferintosh asked.

'That, sir, I will have to judge for myself,' I fenced with words. 'I certainly hope so, Captain. I have no desire to waste my time with a man who is as mundane as everybody else.'

My captain bowed from the waist while still managing to hold my gaze. I could swear that he was laughing at me.

'You said you had two favours,' I reminded. 'May I inquire about the nature of the second?'

'I crave a kiss.' My bold captain told me.

I had hoped for no less. 'A kiss, sir?' I widened my eyes in pretended shock. 'La! I am a lady. I do not part with my kisses lightly.'

'I am glad to hear it,' Captain Ferintosh did not advance one single iota. I had hoped he would rush forward and sweep me off my feet, carry me into the shelter of the cabbage plants and...

'One kiss only,' I ended my fantasy.

'One kiss only.' Captain Ferintosh stepped forward. Placing a hand behind my head, he bent over me. His lips were softer than I had imagined as they touched mine, so lightly that they might have been the feathers of a bird. I responded, pressing back. I had never kissed a man before, except my father and sundry uncles and men who pretended to be uncles. I could feel the hammering of my heart and the harshness of my breathing, yet Captain Ferintosh was so gentle that I need not have been concerned.

'There.' He stepped back, smiling.

'There.' I stepped back with one hand to my throat. I stared at him, not sure what to say or do. It had been a kiss, but not the kiss I had expected. In my mind, kisses were full of passion, with a man's hands holding me tight and his lips pressed firmly against mine. Captain Ferintosh's kiss had not been like that. I wanted more.

'Captain Ferintosh,' I said.

'Yes?' His eyebrows rose. Again, I could have sworn that he was mocking me.

'One kiss is not sufficient,' I said.

'Are you asking for another?'

'I am.'

Captain Ferintosh stepped forward again. This time I knew what to expect and met his lips with my own. I pressed harder than before and slipped my hands around him. You would be right to think me shameless for I felt no shame at all. That man utterly captivated me in ways I still cannot describe. Even now I can feel his hard, lean body as I pulled it closer to me. Even now I can relive the rich aroma of his tobacco.

His hands crept around my shoulders and my waist. Suddenly I was not quite so sure of myself. Captain Ferintosh was now very much in control. His second kiss was as different from his first as a hawk is from a sparrow. His strength was immense, his hands hard as they supported me. I felt lost within his grasp.

When he released me, I was gasping for breath. I did not wish his hands to leave me. I did not wish him to be anywhere but with me.

'Captain Ferintosh!' I could say no more. My throat had closed up. I was trembling. My breathing was ragged. In short, I was a physical and emotional wreck.

'And now, my Lady Mary,' Captain Ferintosh gave a great sweeping bow. 'I must leave you. If you could make your way to Haddington for ten forenoon this next market day, I shall meet you there.'

'People will see us,' I said the first words to come into my head.

'Is that so bad?' Captain Ferintosh asked. 'I would be proud to be seen with you. Would you be ashamed to be seen in my company?'

'No, no,' I struggled to make myself understood. 'I do not mean that at all, Captain. I mean...' I was not sure what I meant. 'My father and mother would come to hear of it. People talk.'

'People do talk,' Captain Ferintosh agreed. 'We will not do anything indecorous.'

I took a deep breath. 'My parents have a man in mind for me. A Mr John Aitken. They would not be pleased to hear of me in the company of another, particularly such a gallant and handsome fellow as you.' *There: it was said.*

Captain Ferintosh took a single step backwards into the shadow of the trees. 'I thank you for your high opinion of me, Lady Mary, and for your honesty.'

I waited for his words of condemnation, for his rejection of such an undutiful daughter as I was proving myself. They did not come.

'Do you have strong feelings for Mr John Aitken?'

I had not expected that question. 'I have never met the gentleman,' I admitted.

'Do you wish to?'

I pondered that. 'Having met Captain Ferintosh, I have no real desire to meet any other gentleman, who would be inferior, I am sure.'

Captain Ferintosh smiled. 'You are a very forthright woman, my Lady Mary.'

'I speak only the truth, sir. I was brought up never to tell a lie, and I am resolved never to do so.' If only I had known then how soon it would be before I came the most accomplished of liars, in deeds if not in words.

'I presume that your parents are hoping for an advantageous marriage with this Mr John Aitken fellow?'

'I presume that is the case,' I said.

'Your father, Mr Andrew Hepburn, is the local JP is he not?'

'That is correct,' I said.

'He is a most respectable man.' Captain Ferintosh glanced toward the house. The walled garden was so situated that it caught the best of the sun, while the walls retained the heat and bounced it back to the plants. With the house being some distance away, we were as safe from observation within the garden as we would be anywhere on my father's lands, unless the gardener appeared.

'My father is the best of men,' I agreed.

'Do you still think him the best of men despite his attempting you into matrimony with an unknown John Aitken?'

'That is one of his little foibles,' I said. 'I am sure he has the best of intentions.' I was not happy with Father, but I would not be disloyal to him.

'It is a very strange foible,' Captain Ferintosh shook his head. 'I do not approve of such things. I think every woman and every man should be free to choose their own path to love, whether that path is conventional or not. Don't you agree, Miss Hepburn?'

'I do agree,' I said. Caught up in the magic of his smile, I would have agreed to virtually anything Captain Ferintosh said.

'Freedom is a noble thing,' Captain Ferintosh repeated my earlier words. 'The freedom to choose, the freedom to live one's life without petty restrictions, the freedom to say what one wants and live with whomever one pleases.' I swear that the captain's eyes were glowing as he spoke.

He certainly convinced me. 'I am a great believer in freedom.'

'Strike off your bonds,' Captain Ferintosh said. 'Meet me at the Mercat Cross in Haddington at ten forenoon.' Bending forward, he kissed me a third time, as if to seal the bargain. 'I promise I will do nothing untoward, Miss Hepburn, and nobody of consequence will even glimpse us together.'

Before I could answer, Captain Ferintosh had stepped back. I did not see him leave the walled garden yet when Mr Mitchell wandered in, pushing a squeaking wheelbarrow, the place was deserted.

Chapter Four

It is never easy for a young woman to travel alone. There are so many restrictions, whether or not she intends to meet a man of whom her parents would be unlikely to approve. In such situations, one must resort to subterfuge, if not downright lies. Now, I am no great believer in falsehoods of any kind, but I was so enamoured with Captain Ferintosh that I spun a web of fabrication purely to see him again. I wonder how many young women, or young men, have not done similar when courting?

I was fortunate that I had a most particular friend in Catherine Brown. Catherine was the daughter of Archibald Brown of Laverockhill, a most respectable farmer who Father knew well. Catherine was a brown-haired, brown-eyed woman of my own age and the most amiable disposition it was possible to imagine. That very afternoon, I sent a servant with a note to Catherine; she returned the favour before evening, and after a flurry of note-exchanging that must have exhausted the servants, I had the arrangements in place.

'I would like to visit Haddington Market,' I said, quite truthfully, to Father as we sat to our evening meal.

'Why?' Mother was instantly suspicious.

'I have a particular friend who asked me to go there.' I said, still truthfully.

'Archie Brown told me that Catherine expressed a similar interest,' Father smiled over his legal papers. 'I wonder if she could be your particular friend.'

I felt Mother's relief.

'She has been my particular friend for many years,' I agreed. So you see, I did not tell a single lie but acted a complete falsehood.

'Take Coffee,' Mother said, referring to her horse, which happened to be a favourite of mine.

'Thank you, Mother,' I dropped into an unnecessary curtsey.

'There is little enough for young girls to do in the country,' Mother continued. 'A trip to the market is as harmless a diversion as one can imagine.'

'When you are there,' Father looked up briefly from his papers. 'Check the prices for wheat and barley would you?'

That was all that was said, except the expected warnings to be careful and keep together.

I will not bore you with details of our ride across country to Haddington. Suffice to say that Catherine was wild with excitement to hear my reasons. I had known Catherine all my life, and we trusted each other with our most intimate secrets. I told her about Captain Ferintosh, leaving nothing unsaid. I may possibly have exaggerated some aspects a little. Not much, just sufficient to titillate and tease poor Catherine, leaving her in a state of agitated suspense.

'You are a bad woman,' Catherine spoke with the sort of heat that only envy can produce.

'I know.' I said. 'What will you do when I am with the captain?'

'I will sit in the coffee house,' Catherine said. 'I will drink coffee by myself and mourn the absence of my most particular friend, who prefers the company of a stranger to mine.'

'Good,' I knew that Catherine was teasing. 'That means you will sit in a coffee shop hoping to be admired by only the most handsome of men.'

We laughed together as only old friends can. I salved my conscience by telling myself that Catherine had a hundred cousins all across East

Lothian including three in Haddington. She would never want for company.

I had never felt such excitement as I waited for Captain Ferintosh. The market at Haddington was busy with farmers selling and buying cattle, farm labourers lounging, drinking, wenching or chatting, and scores of beasts, carts and children creating mayhem. Catherine stood nearby, eager for a sight of the gallant captain. When I tried to wave her away, she merely waved back, the minx.

'My Lady Mary.'

Again, I did not see Captain Ferintosh appear. One moment I was searching for him amidst the surging tide of farming humanity, the next he was at my side, resplendent in a blue cutaway coat above a buff waistcoat, with skin-tight breeches that left little to my imagination. The weak sun glittered on the gold braid that adorned his tricorne cat.

'You are dressed for a city ball,' I looked down at my own, more practical, or perhaps more mundane, appearance. 'I look dowdy in comparison.'

'You could wear rags and still outshine King Louis of France and all the court of Versailles,' Captain Ferintosh gave a sweeping bow that attracted the attention of some half-dozen women.

'Have you been to France?' I was determined to find out all that I could about my captain. 'You never talk about yourself, Captain Ferintosh.'

'I have been to France,' Captain Ferintosh said. 'It is not what you expect.' He lowered his voice conspiratorially. 'It was raining,' he said, 'and full of Frenchmen.'

The captain took my arm and guided me away from the ancient Mercat Cross. Fortunately, it was a dry day, or we would both be spattered with mud from the farm carts, even as it was we had to walk circumspectly to avoid what the animals left behind.

'Where are you taking me?' I looked around for Catherine, who waved again. 'You are certainly not dressed to spend time in Haddington Market.'

'You are correct,' Captain Ferintosh said. 'I told you that I would not damage your respectability, I have a carriage with me. Where would you like to go?'

I was not sure. 'Somewhere romantic,' I said without thought. 'My horse is in the stables.'

'Coffee will be safe there.' Trust the captain to know the name of my horse. 'And Catherine Brown of Laverockhill will be equally safe without you.' He lowered his voice to a conspiratorial whisper. 'I have instructed one of my men to watch over her.'

That sounded immensely thrilling. I felt a shiver of delight run down my spine. 'One of your men? Do you mean one of the crew from your ship, Captain?'

'I mean you should not worry about your friend,' Captain Ferintosh said. 'She is as safe as if she was at home. She will also find a sovereign soon...'

I turned to watch Mary and, sure enough, she bent over to pick up something from the ground. She held the golden coin, looking bemused as Captain Ferintosh smiled and twirled his cane. 'There now. Catherine can eat and drink like a queen today. You need not think of her again.'

'You are a kind and generous man,' I said. I wondered if Catherine would enjoy the company of a strange man, or if she would find one of her cousins.

'Others may not agree,' Captain Ferintosh said. 'Now, what kind of romantic destination would you like?'

I had recently read Walpole's *The Castle of Otranto*, and Reeve's *The Old English Baron*, so my taste was leaning toward gothic romance. 'Take me to a castle,' I said, thinking of the fairy-tale castles of the Rhine or the recently-mentioned King of France's palace of Versailles.

If you know East Lothian, you will know that it is a county steeped in history. We have battle sites galore, from Dunbar where Edward Longshanks of England smashed the Scottish chivalry to Prestonpans where Bonnie Charles Stewart scattered the redcoats and Johnnie Cope was first to carry news of his own defeat to anxious Hanoverians. We have places such as Athelstaneford where the Scottish Saltire appeared in the sky to inspire a patriot army to defeat the invading Angles and Traprain Law where old Lot of Lothian had his capital. We also have a plethora of castles. As a small selection, there is Dunbar, where Black Agnes withstood a siege, Dirleton with its bowling green and courtyard and Tantallon, my particular favourite. 'Ding doon Tantallon,' goes the rhyme, 'build a bridge to the Bass,' which were two things thought of as impossible in the old days. Well, Tantallon has been well dinged doon, leaving the most romantic of ruins.

'Take me to Tantallon,' I said.

'Tantallon it is.' Captain Ferintosh assented.

I did not know what to expect when the captain told me he had his own carriage, but certainly nothing as luxurious as the chariot to which he led me. If the captain's clothes were opulent, then his carriage was undoubtedly regal.

Gilded in gold, the dark body had its own coat of arms and a pair of matching chocolate-brown stallions. There was even a coachman in matching green and yellow.

'Who are you, Captain?' I asked in some awe. 'Am I in the presence of royalty?'

'Nothing so exalted,' Captain Ferintosh said.

'A duke, perhaps?'

'Not even a duke,' Captain Ferintosh shook his head. The coachman jumped from his perch to open the door and let down the step for us both. He was a handsome enough fellow as well in his tight breeches.

'An earl?' I worked my way down the social scale step by step.

'Not even close,' Captain Ferintosh lent me his arm to clamber inside the coach. The interior was of rich, soft green leather with a rug on the floor in place of the usual straw.

'A lord then?' I sank into the cushioned seat and took hold of the leather strap that a careful designer had provided to ensure passengers were not knocked all a-tumble when the coach rounded sharp corners.

'Not a lord nor a knight nor even a baron,' Captain Ferintosh slid opposite me, grinning. 'I have no title except Captain and no noble line of any sort.'

'Oh.' I am not sure if I was disappointed or not. You will know that in my day, many young women aspired to marry a title. The daughters of rich manufacturers or merchants polished their education in finishing schools and sallied forth to balls and gatherings in the hope of meeting a member of the social elite. Penniless lords obtained a fortune in exchange for a wedding ring, and merchant's daughters found social acceptance for themselves and their children merely by warming the bed of their titled husband. Love was not always expected. What happened outside the confines of the marriage was nobody's business as long as it was kept quiet. Nobody wanted a scandal of course, so wives turned a blind eye to the amorous affairs of their husbands and presumed that their husbands would allow them to live their own physical lives once the duty of producing an heir or two had been successfully negotiated.

I did not wish such a false, hollow life. That is why I broke my mother's cardinal rule of stepping into the carriage of a man I barely knew. I sought romance in my life as well as a comfortable marriage, and in my book, both should be tied in the same man. Call me an idealist if you wish, but that was my dream, and with Captain Ferintosh, both seemed possible. Was I taking a chance? Yes. Was I aware of the risks and the ruination of my reputation and life? Yes, but youth is eternally optimistic. The evil that befalls others will never befall us, or so we believe.

'Now tell me, Lady Mary,' Captain Ferintosh said. 'If you saw me in this carriage, 'would you think I was the scion of a noble house?' He smiled at me across the interior of the carriage. 'You are a gentlewoman born and bred. What would you believe?'

'What a strange question,' I said. 'I don't believe I've ever been asked anything so queer in my life before.'

'Well, Lady Mary?'

I sat back, smiling as I considered Captain Ferintosh. 'I think you are the most perfect gentleman,' I said. 'I only wonder why you were walking across Lammermuir dressed like a gentleman at large in the city.'

'I will settle for the most perfect gentleman,' Captain Ferintosh glanced out of the window. 'Do recognise where we are?'

'I have lived in East Lothian all my life,' I said. 'I know we are on the road between Haddington and North Berwick.'

'Do you know the people as well?' Captain Ferintosh's gaze never left my face. 'I suppose you will. Your father is an important man.'

'I know the local farmers,' I said. 'I know some of the lairds and gentry.'

'Who would you say is the most important landowner in your corner of the county?' Captain Ferintosh leaned back. 'There now, Lady Mary; there is a quiz for you.'

I pondered for a moment. 'There is no major landowner,' I said. 'Many are tenants of the Duke of Buccleuch, who lives at Dalkeith Palace and not in East Lothian. Others have a couple of hundred acres, like my father.'

'Is there not a lord or an earl in the area?'

'There is Lady Emily Hume,' I said. 'Lady Emily of Huntlaw House is the closest we have to a great landowner.'

'That's the lady,' Captain Ferintosh said. 'I have heard she is a bit of a recluse.'

'She is,' I said. 'I don't think anybody has met her face-to-face for years.'

Captain Ferintosh seemed satisfied with that information. 'Here we are at the castle,' he said. 'Come on, Lady Mary.'

I said that Tantallon was my favourite of all East Lothian's Castles, and with reason. Set on the coast, it commands the most spectacular views over the Firth of Forth, with the great white lump of the Bass Rock and the distant Isle of May.

Captain Ferintosh dismounted and gave his hand to help me out before ordering the driver to open the boot and bring out what was inside.

'May I help?' I asked.

'Absolutely not,' Captain Ferintosh said. 'Pray allow us to prepare things.'

Somehow the captain's man had managed to fold up a chair in the boot, which he now produced for me. I sat there in state, like the Queen of France, or is it the Empress of France nowadays? Or are they reduced to a republic again? I do find the constant changes of these Continental potentates so tiresome, as must you. Why don't they make their minds up for one thing or another? It makes little difference to ordinary people. We pay our taxes and grumble at how bad things are compared to our younger days. As far as I can see, one ruler is every bit as useless as another although our present young queen seems to be an exception.

As it sat there, watching the men work, seagulls wheeled and circled around the great red walls of Tantallon. I thought of the old days when the Douglases controlled this castle and Scots and English and kings and nobles fought for control. All done with now and we're all friends together and nobody one whit the better for all the raw blood spilt.

'Are you ready, Lady Mary?' Captain Ferintosh lent me his arm.

I had never seen anything quite like the spread Captain Ferintosh had prepared. He and his man had worked wonders to erect a table and two chairs, although where they had secreted it away on the coach, I could not begin to guess. A crisp white tablecloth covered the table, with all sorts of delicacies set on bone china tableware that would put the royal household to shame.

'Wherever did you find so many rarities?' I asked. I could not even name the exotic fruits and meats that covered the table.

'For you, my Lady, 'Captain Ferintosh pulled out my chair with a flourish. 'I have travelled the world.'

We started with some bubbling French champagne, which was like drinking frothy water, although I did not tell Captain Ferintosh that for fear of hurting his feelings. I could not tell you what we ate and drank that day, only that the captain treated me like a queen. Perhaps I am the last person to be banqueted at Tantallon Castle. I do not know.

I do know that Captain Ferintosh acted like a perfect host as well as a perfect gentleman.

Once we had dined, the captain ordered his man to clear everything away while he took me on a perambulation around the ancient walls. Or rather wall, for Tantallon is a strange sort of castle. It is built on a promontory, with cliffs descending to the sea on three sides and a massive curtain wall on the landward face. I presume that there were walls on the seaward sides at one time, but if so, nothing much now remains.

'Do you like your domain, Lady Mary?' Captain Ferintosh took my arm in the crook of his elbow.

After the champagne and claret, I felt as if I was floating on air. 'I like it a great deal.'

We halted at the edge of the cliff, with the great breakers crashing on the beach below. 'I wish to ask you another strange question, my Lady. Are you ready?'

'Ask anything you wish, Captain.' I was happy to lean against him in the strong wind. I wondered what my mother would say if she saw me now, being wined, dined and wooed by such a gallant gentleman.

'I know you are from a respectable background,' Captain Ferintosh seemed to be sounding me out again. I wondered if he was ascertaining if I was suitable marriage material for a man of his standing. I hid my smile; my mother could keep her plain John Aitken.

'Yes,' I agreed, waiting for the captain's next words.

'Is your father also rich?'

Well, that was blatant. 'In other words, do I come with a dowry?' The words left my mouth before I could stop them.

'No, my Lady,' Fortunately, Captain Ferintosh did not take offence. 'If our friendship developed to the extent that I considered matrimony, I would not need a dowry. I am, let us say, a man of independent means.'

'Oh,' I felt very foolish. 'Then pray, why do you ask?'

The captain smiled. 'You are a young lady of exquisite manners and considerable decorum, Lady Mary. Normally wealth alone brings such poise. I was attempting to ascertain if, in your case, it was natural.'

I laughed. 'My father is not a wealthy man, Captain. The farm pays its way with little margin or leeway.'

'In that case,' Captain Ferintosh bowed, 'your poise is entirely natural and all the more commendable for that.'

'And you, sir?' I tried to steer the conversation away from me and onto a more interesting subject. 'You still have neglected to tell me your name, or where you are from.'

'I am a child of the world,' Captain Ferintosh twirled his cane, 'and I have many names.'

Well, that may be very romantic, but it did not help me in the slightest. 'I cannot continue to call you Captain,' I said, rather too hotly. 'You must have a given name.'

'Will Captain not be sufficient for now?'

'No,' I said. 'I feel as if you don't trust me.' I pulled away from his hand. Oh, I was quite prepared to have him leave me there, stranded at Tantallon, miles from home. I could walk to North Berwick, hire a post-chaise and find my way to Coffee at Haddington. I was not quite as green as I acted.

'My kindly parents named me Edmund,' Captain Ferintosh said. 'There now, can you blame me for hiding my name? Edmund Ferintosh.' He bowed. 'At your service.'

That was more like it. 'Edmund Ferintosh. There is nothing wrong with your name; nothing at all.' It was unusual, and all the better for that.

Captain Ferintosh shook his head. 'There is nothing wrong with my name until you have to live with it. Edmund Ferintosh is a bit of a mouthful.' Retaking my arm, he led me back to the coach. 'Could you imagine it, Lady Mary, Mrs Edmund Ferintosh? How would you like it, then?'

The breath caught in my throat at the name. *Mrs Edmund Ferintosh.* 'It is a fine name,' I said. *Had that been a marriage proposal? Was the captain asking me to marry him in a uniquely oblique manner? Was this entire day been to prepare me for that question?* My heart hammered within my chest as I wondered. *Was I ready for marriage? Was I prepared to marry this bold, mysterious gallant man with all his finery?* These questions filled my mind as we travelled back to Haddington.

'You are very quiet.' Captain Ferintosh said as we pulled up outside the stables.

'I have a lot on my mind,' I left the chariot in a flurry of skirts.

'Have you enjoyed your day?' Captain Ferintosh asked. I wondered if he would kiss me farewell in front of half of Haddington. I hoped not; the day was now drawing toward evening, the light was fading, and some of the more rowdy elements of the town were making their presence heard.

'I have enjoyed my day,' I did not forget to curtsey. 'I thank you for your hospitality, Captain.' I lowered my voice. 'Or Edmund, rather.'

'I do prefer Captain. I dislike that Edmund name intensely.'

We had that in common then. 'Captain Ferintosh it is.' I put a hand on his sleeve. 'Thank you for letting me into your confidence, Captain.' I hesitated, not sure what to say.

Thankfully Captain Ferintosh spared me the trouble. 'I know I can trust you, Lady Mary. There are very few people I can say that about. I can trust you with my name.'

I can trust you with my name. Was that another insinuation? Was the captain again hinting at me becoming Mrs Ferintosh?

Before I had time to reply, Captain Ferintosh lifted his hand in farewell. The driver whipped up, and the coach jolted away. I watched until it was clear of the market.

Mrs Captain Edmund Ferintosh. The name echoed inside my head. I thought of a lifetime of luxurious coaches and sumptuous meals in romantic locations. *Mrs Edmund Ferintosh: was such a thing possible?*

'Well now,' I had not seen Catherine lingering in the shadow of the Cross. 'That's a fancy chariot for a man you are going to tell me all about.'

'His name is Captain Ferintosh,' I said.

'And?' Catherine raised her eyebrows. 'You already told me that much.'

I attempted a mysterious smile, as women do in all the best romantic novels.

'You're not going to say any more, are you?' Catherine said. 'You are the most infuriating of women, Mary Hepburn.'

'Thank you,' I mocked her with a curtsey.

'Come on now, Mary,' Catherine said. 'We'd better get back before full dark.'

The entire ride home, I thought about Captain Ferintosh's words, trying to work out what he had been trying to tell me. He could have been hinting at a future marriage proposal, or he might not. Now I had another dilemma. There was a very amiable man requesting my hand in marriage, while my mother had quite another gentleman in mind for me. Now, despite my youth and apparent naivety, I was sensible enough to realise that Captain Edmund Ferintosh was not all he seemed. Charming gentlemen in beautiful clothes did not habitually enjoy a stroll across boggy muirland; nor did men assume the title of captain unless they had either commanded a ship or had military experience. My captain's hands were too soft for any seaman who worked with tarry ropes, while he had not shown any inclination to discuss military matters. Captain Ferintosh was a rogue, albeit a very amiable rogue.

I liked him. I liked him a lot. I thought about him every day. I tried not to think about Mr John Aitken. When I did, I had the most horrible palpitations. If I were a horse, I would say that I broke out in a cold sweat. As I was a lady, I will say I glowed. Profusely.

Three days later, my situation altered again, quite dramatically.

Chapter Five

I had never seen Father look so serious. He took the pistol from the drawer in which it had resided for many months, laid it on the table in front of him and began to clean it. I watched with some apprehension.

'Father, what are you doing?'

He looked up. 'Cleaning my pistol,' his smile was forced. 'Don't look so worried, Mary. It's only a precaution. I doubt I'll need it.'

'Father,' I asked. 'Where are you going? Why are you taking a gun? You never carry a gun.'

'Hold that will you?' Father asked. 'It's not easy loading with only one hand.'

I held the heavy, old-fashioned pistol as he loaded it, tamping down the powder and rolling in the ball before ramming down the wad to keep it secure.

'Do you remember these whisky smugglers I had before me on the bench the other day?'

'Yes; the scoundrels.'

'That's the ones.' Father looked surprised that I had remembered any details of his work. 'I questioned them before the trial to see if I could learn any more about their operations. They asked if I would give them a lighter sentence if they told me the location of their leader.'

'Did you allow such a thing?' I wondered.

'I did,' Father said. 'I am now going to arrest their leader.'

'Can you trust them, father? Will the scoundrels tell the truth?'

'If they mislead me,' Father had never sounded grimmer. 'They will regret it, I assure you.'

I held up the pistol. It was heavier than I expected. 'Will it be dangerous?'

Father took the pistol from me. He placed it on the table, where it lay, sinister, a reminder of the ugly side of life outside the confines of Cauldneb. 'Do you remember our conversation about a king of crime?'

I nodded, wordless.

'If this man is who I hope he is.' Father said, 'he may be in that category.'

'Father!' I did not want to point out the obvious.

'I know,' Father said. 'I only have one arm.' This time his smile looked more genuine. 'I am not going alone, Mary.'

I tried to smile. 'I should hope not, Father.'

'I have sent word to all our neighbours.' Father said. 'East Lothian is about to become lively.'

The first man arrived at Cauldneb half an hour later. James Flockhart came as if he was going to fight the French, with a pair of horse pistols at his saddle as well as a fowling piece strapped across his back. A rangy man in his thirties, Mr Flockhart was also a dedicated sportsman who knew how to handle his firearms. Elliot of Muirhead was next, a hard-faced man with a single pistol, followed by a middle-aged, balding man I did not know.

'Who is that?' I asked.

'That's Mr John Aitken of Tyneford,' Mother said.

I felt as if somebody had thrown a bucket of cold water over me. 'Mr John Aitken?' I studied the man that my loving parents thought would be a suitable match for me. He was of middle height, gasped as he rode and sat his saddle like a sack of potatoes. This ageing dotard was the fellow my mother said shared my tastes. When I compared John Aitken to Captain Ferintosh, I thought how wrong my parents were. While the captain was vigorous, handsome, dashing and decidedly romantic, Mr John Aitken was none of these things. Appalled, I looked away and shook my head.

Dear Heavens, Mother. Do you honestly believe that I could even be friends with an old man like that? Captain Ferintosh looked ever more appealing.

'What's to do?' I tried desperately to force my mind onto other matters. 'Why is everybody carrying guns? Is this fellow the leader of a band of desperadoes like the Hawkshurst Gang?' The Hawkshurst gang had been a bunch of murderous rogues who had created mayhem in southern England. We did not have their like in Scotland.

'We hope not.' Father checked the priming of his pistol before tucking it away in a holster. His smile was intended to reassure me. I refused to be comforted.

'If he is,' John Aitken's voice was like a rusty hinge, creaking as he spoke. 'If he is, we'll lay him by the heels and drag him back at the tail of a horse.'

James Flockhart looked at me, steady-eyed. 'Now, don't you fret, Miss Hepburn. We'll catch the rogue and keep him safe and sound. We know the area better than anybody living.'

I felt my heart flutter inside me. 'Thank you, Mr Flockhart. Father; take care. Don't be taking any chances.'

'I won't.' Father said.

'Your father knows what he's doing.' Mother looked as calm as if her husband was merely riding to market rather than venturing on some quasi-military expedition. She was at her best at times like this; bless her rock-solid devotion to what was right and proper.

'What can I do to help?' I looked around, feeling helpless.

'There are some men still missing,' Mother said at once. 'They've probably got lost coming here. See if you can find them.'

That was definite and precise. I had the stable lad saddle Coffee, mounted her and trotted out of Cauldneb's policies to find the missing riders. It was not the most important of tasks, but one that kept me occupied rather than worrying about Father and, incidentally, thinking about Mr John Aitken, who I already viewed as a horrible old man.

'It's that way, I say!'

'No! You're wrong. That's Cauldneb up there.'

'We've already passed it.'

I heard the argument only five minutes after I left our grounds. The three men all pointed in different directions, with only one indicating the path to Cauldneb.

'Good morning gentlemen,' I interrupted their discussion. 'Are you looking for Mr Hepburn's property?'

'We are.' The man who had been correct was first to speak. He was a slightly dishevelled, dark-haired fellow with a ready smile.

'In that case, gentlemen, if you would care to follow me, I will lead you right there.'

'Wait now,' a blond-haired young gallant pulled his horse beside Coffee. His name was George Aberdare, and I had known him all my life. 'Wait, I said. We are gentlemen. Do we jump when a woman tells us to?'

'Only when she is correct, George,' the dishevelled man said.

'I don't think she is correct, Colligere,'

I sighed. 'Listen, gentlemen. I am heading back to Cauldneb. If you choose to follow me, you will be going the right way.' Turning Coffee around, I headed home. I had no patience with stupid men, and George Aberdare was just that. I heard the sound of only two horses behind me.

'Most people call me Alexander,' the dishevelled one introduced himself with a short bow from the saddle. 'How de do.'

'Mary Hepburn,' I bobbed as best I could.

'His name is Alexander Colligere,' the second man tapped his head with a long forefinger and pointed to Alexander. He lowered his voice to a very audible whisper. 'He's a bit lacking, don't you know?'

I looked at Alexander Colligere, expecting some retaliation. Instead, he smiled and looked away. *A bit shy then*, I thought.

'You must be Mr Andrew Aitken's daughter,' the second man said. 'I'm Wattie Ormiston.'

'How do you do, Mr Ormiston,' I was not sure if I liked him after his barbed introduction of Alexander Colligere.

George Aberdare galloped up behind us a moment later. 'This is the right way, after all, hang it.' He gave me a broad grin. 'Halloa, Mary I did not recognise you there.'

'Good morning, George.' Only George could ride past a gate he had entered through at least a score of times. I allowed him to follow behind us without any more ado. Anybody who was so stupid deserved no more attention from me. I will try not to mention George Aberdare again.

Mr Ormiston rode at my side, with Mr Colligere lagging behind.

'Are you all right, Mr Colligere?' I asked. I felt sorry for the fellow if Mr Ormiston and the stupid Aberdare were the best companions he had. There! I promised to try not to mention Aberdare again, and I have done so. Promises are such fragile things.

'Yes, thank you,' Mr Colligere said. 'You have some magnificent trees in your policies.'

'Thank you, Mr Colligere. My father is rather proud of them.' I warmed a little to Mr Colligere. Any man who appreciated trees must have a good streak in him, even if he was, in Mr Ormiston's words 'a bit lacking.'

I left Mr Colligere to admire the trees while I ushered the others into the withdrawing room, where Mother and Jeannie, our housekeeper, were busy fortifying them with food for the day ahead. Men need to be fed at all times, Mother often informed me, and ensured that she was at the forefront in the feeding process. Cook must have been busy that day. The withdrawing room was equally busy with all the men discussing their plans while Father moved around, everybody's friend although very much in charge.

'Who are they pursuing, Mother? It must surely be the King of France, or the Young Pretender returned from the dead or some such villain.' Charles Edward Stuart had won one of his victories at nearby Prestonpans, so he had been an ogre of our childhood, although the Jacobite threat passed decades before.

'It must surely be a great rogue,' Mother agreed. I could see the worry in her eyes beneath the smile of the hostess. 'Father does not discuss such things with me.'

That was the other side of Father, you see. Legal business was man's work. Women were excluded. It was the way of the world and still is in many households. I resolved that when and if I were married, my husband would not exclude me from that critical part of his life. That resolution edged my mind back to thoughts of John Aitken and Captain Ferintosh. My excitement at seeing such a great host in Cauldneb dissipated. I looked surreptitiously at John Aitken, with the candle-light reflecting from his balding head.

Oh Dear Lord. Am I to be married to that?

I listened as his rusty-gate voice creaked across the room, shuddered and wished that Captain Ferintosh had driven me to his non-existent ship yesterday and sailed away to the Americas, or Hindustan or some other wondrous place of colour and excitement.

'Go and serve our guests,' Mother urged. 'I see that Mr Aitken has joined us.' Well, she already knew that! Mother lowered her voice. 'Pay particular attention to him, Mary. Try and make a good impression.' She dropped her voice to a whisper. 'Do try to keep control of your temper!'

'Yes, Mother.' I drifted back to the guests, bobbed in a curtsey to Mr Colligere, who had managed to tear his attention from our trees, and ignored Mr Aitken as if he carried the plague. Mr Ormiston was paying his respects to a tray of Jeannie's cakes.

'These are devilishly good,' Mr Ormiston said. 'I must ask your cook for the recipe. My wife has an astounding love of sweet things.'

'I rather like the sound of your wife, Mr Ormiston,' I said, hoping that he was less acid-tongued with her than he had been with poor Mr Colligere.

'What the devil!' I turned at the shout and crash to see two men sprawled on the floor. John Aitken and Alexander Colligere had some-how managed to bump into each other, unbalancing both. Mr Aitken lay on his face, blaspheming fit to frighten the French, while Mr Colligere was laughing as if life was a great joke. I have to forgive myself for hoping that Mr Aitken was hurt. Ignoring him, I lifted my skirts and crouched beside Mr Colligere.

'Are you all right, sir? I trust that you are uninjured.'

'Right as the day is long,' Mr Colligere said. He stood up without my help. 'It was only a tumble.'

'You careless young snipe!' John Aitken had his own dash of temper, I noticed. Well, he had better not try to unleash it on me, or he'll find he has gripped the devil by the tail. 'What the devil do you think you were doing? By God, I've a mind to...'

'Are you injured, Mr Aitken?' Mother cut off his blustering rhetoric with practised words while the other men watched and grinned, thinking the entire affair a colossal joke.

'No,' Mr Aitken calmed down under Mother's administrations. 'I spilt my drink though. Damned young whippersnapper.'

'Here we are,' Mother found a glass of French brandy. You will notice that, magistrate or not, Father had no objections to imbibing with smuggled brandy. We lived by double standards, you see. I am sure he allowed some petty criminals go scot-free as well, although he was hard on others.

'Well, gentlemen,' Father spoke above the hubbub. 'If we are all assembled, I think we should be on our way. The day is wearing on.'

'Our quarry won't remain in the same den all day,' Mr Flockhart lifted a hunting horn to his lips. Only Mother's practised frown prevented him from blowing it inside the house. Some things are just not done in Cauldneb.

The men clattered outside with great noise and laughter. One would think they were engaged on some sporting occasion rather than hunting a no-doubt desperate scoundrel. Men are like that; they like to put sport before all things.

I watched them ride out. Father was in the lead, riding as well with his single arm as any of the others with two. James Flockhart was behind him, with John Aitken sitting like a lump of lard at his back, then came Elliot of Muirhead, James Flockhart, Anderson of Langdyke, and Brown of Laverockhill, Catherine's father. Except for John Aitken, Ormiston and the strange Alexander Colligere, all were local gentlemen I had known all my life, quiet, hard-grafting men of the soil, church-goers with wives and families, not wild men to ride into battle.

'I don't like this, Mother,' I said.

'Men do what has to be done,' Mother put her hand on my shoulder. 'It has always been. Come now, we have a house to run.'

I watched the riders' dust slowly settle onto the ground. Somewhere a cock crowed, with a gaggle of hens cackling shortly afterwards. A dog barked, once, twice and again. I remained at the doorway, feeling that my life was about to change. I don't know why I felt like that; perhaps it was because of the turning of the year with autumn crisping the leaves and clouds gathering above the German Ocean behind the great white lump of the Bass Rock.

'Mary,' Mother called. 'Watching won't bring them home any the quicker. Work is the answer. Work occupies the mind and the body.'

Mother had a simple solution to most matters. Work. We worked while waiting for Father. For all her words about a servant's work, Mother could scrub, polish and clean with the best of them. She led the way while I followed, pretending not to notice the way she looked out of the window every few minutes and started up at every sound that could be her man coming home. I knew my mother, you see, the good and the better of her. I could not understand why she should choose a man such as John Aitken for me.

'Mother,' I asked. 'Why John Aitken?'

'John Aitken is a fine young man,' Mother said. 'But this is hardly the time to discuss him.'

'He's hardly young,' I said.

'He's a little older than you, true,' Mother said.

'Quite a lot older,' I retorted with more force than I intended.

Mother smiled. 'When you grow older, age matters less. Why, your father is quite a few years older than I am.'

'Only a few years,' I thought of John Aitken's balding head and decided paunch. 'Not very many.'

'There, you see?' Mother smiled at me across the floor we were scrubbing. 'Not very many. Your father and I jog along very nicely, don't we?'

'Yes, Mother,' I agreed, 'but John Aitken!'

'You'll like him when you meet him properly,' Mother said. 'Now, I don't want to hear another word on the subject. Not one word!' She raised her finger to signify that the discussion was closed.

I spent the majority of that day thinking of the candlelight gleaming on Mr John Aitken's balding head, his sudden flare of temper at placid Alexander Colligere and his rotund body. Comparing him with Captain Ferintosh, I felt a mixture of despair and anger.

No, I told myself. *I will not marry that old man. I will not even contemplate marriage to that old man. I will run away, rather than that!*

Run away where? I asked myself in a moment of sanity. Where could a lone woman escape to? We were not like men. We could not sign on a whaling ship, or join the army, or run away to the Hudson's Bay or the East India Company. Perhaps I could emigrate to Canada or the new United States? As what? A lone woman with no fortune? The very best I could hope for was a servant's position or perhaps a governess, and then only if I could afford the passage, or indentured myself for seven years.

I shuddered. I was trapped in my woman's body, condemned by my own mother.

'They're coming back, Mrs Hepburn.' Jeannie stood in the doorway shading her eyes from the evening sun. 'Mr Hepburn is leading, and nobody is missing.'

'Oh, thank the Lord.' Mother's words revealed something of the anxiety she had been feeling. Rising at once, she pulled at my sleeve. 'Come, Mary. Come and welcome your father home.'

'The mess…' I glanced at the floor with its pails of water, discarded scrubbing brushes and cakes of hard soap.

'Leave it. That's why we have servants.'

Father led the riders at walking pace. The men looked weary, covered in dust and froth from the horses. In the middle of them was a horse I thought was empty until I realised there was a man tied across the middle, face down.

Ignoring him, I ran to Father. I made a point of avoiding John Aitken, who looked balder, older and fatter than ever.

'Andrew.' Mother walked sedately across the cobbles in front of our house, as if she had not been worried sick the last few hours. 'I'm glad to see you back.'

'Thank you, my dear.' Stiff after so long in the saddle, Father dismounted. His smile was tired. 'We got the man we were after. This fellow,' he gestured to the man tied across the spare horse, 'has been organising the whisky stills all across the county and beyond. We don't know what other mischief he has been up to.'

'Is he dangerous?' Mother squinted at the prisoner as if willing to hang him there and then.

'He might have been,' Father said. 'My informants were most helpful in telling me where he was located. We rounded him up.'

'You had to fire your pistol.' Observant Mother pointed to the powder stains on Father's sleeve.

'Yes.' One word. 'It will wash.' Father tugged at the reins of the spare horse. 'I'll take this fellow to Muirend lock up for the night. We'll have him in the townhouse jail in Haddington tomorrow.'

'Are you going to eat first?' Mother asked.

'I'll eat when I come back,' Father said. 'We won't be long.'

'Come on, you; time to go to the lockup.' John Aitken gave the prisoner a hearty whack with his riding whip. The man jerked his head up, and for one shocking instant, I found myself staring into the dark eyes of Captain Ferintosh.

Chapter Six

'Oh, dear Lord!'

I looked away quickly as a hundred emotions surged through my body. I do not know which was uppermost. Alarm that my captain should be on the other side of the law, fear for his future, sick dread that he might be hanged or transported, anger at my father and his friends for capturing Captain Ferintosh and treating him in such a manner, or sorrow to see him in such a plight.

'Are you all right, Mary?' Mother had noticed my reaction.

I tried to compose myself. 'Yes, Mother, thank you.' I stepped back as Father and John Aitken led their prisoner away. I had to find space by myself. I could not think with so many people present. Some of the other gentlemen were looking curiously at me.

'Don't you worry about him, Miss Hepburn,' Elliot had completely misconstrued my agitation. 'He won't be able to harm you.'

'Is that what the matter was?' Alexander Colligere leaned forward in his saddle. 'I thought Miss Hepburn was looking concerned. Don't you fret, Miss Hepburn. He's tied up safe.'

Unable to say more, I lifted my skirt, turned and walked away with as much dignity as I could muster.

Usually, I would head for the walled garden, but with night drawing on I knew Mother would follow me there and chivvy me inside. Fortunately, we had a small library set on the topmost floor. I hurried there, skipping up the stairs with my feet clicking and clacking and my skirt rustling like the sails of a ship in a fluky breeze.

Only when I entered the library and stood with my back to the door did I allow my emotions to surface. I stood there, sobbing, with my breath coming in deep gasps and my legs trembling. I did not know what to do.

Was there some mistake? Was Captain Ferintosh some black scoundrel that needed so many armed men to hunt him down? Or was he an innocent man accused by others intent on his downfall? Who would do that to my gallant captain? Who would possibly wish to harm such a handsome, elegant, amiable gentleman?

I tried to think back to what Father had said. What had put him on the track of the captain? It had been the two scoundrels Father had in custody for whisky smuggling. I took a deep breath. That might be Simmy and Peter, the two men Captain Ferintosh had rescued me from. Had they taken their revenge by falsely accusing the captain?

Unconscious of what I was doing, I began to pace the length of the library, which did not take long as it was a comparatively small room. It was also growing very dark, as I discovered when I stumbled over a small coffee-table, turned and fell over the blasted thing again. I kicked it aside in my temper, hurt my toe and said some words that no young lady should know.

If these two scoundrels were the cause of placing the captain in jail, then I was also involved, as he had crossed them by helping me. I had to reciprocate. I had to help Captain Ferintosh. I wanted to help him. The thoughts crammed into my mind, jumbling and tumbling over one another as I paced the short length of the library, alternatively tripping over the coffee table and barking my shins off its top. Honestly, one would think I would have the sense to light a candle. However, misery does not allow reason to share its space, and I wallowed in wretchedness even as I wrestled with the problem I convinced myself was entirely my fault.

If I had not been so inquisitive, I would not have come across that illicit still. If I had not come across the still, Peter and Simmy would not have caught me. If Peter and Simmy had not caught me, Captain Ferintosh would not have had to rescue me. If Captain Ferintosh had not saved me, Simmy and Peter would not have clyped on him to my father. The fault lay squarely at my door. It was up to me to restore the situation.

I stopped at the window, looking out over the autumn-dark East Lothian countryside. I loved that view, with the tiny pinpricks of light from the scattered cottages and villages across the plain, to the riding lights of the ships that sat at anchor out on the Forth. Down there, in that dim cluster of lights that marked the village of Kirkton of Muirend, my friend and companion Captain Ferintosh lay in the village lockup, awaiting transport to Haddington Jail, trial and possible exile or worse, and it was all my fault.

Taking a deep breath, I resolved to do something about it.

Adjusting my dress and tidying my hair, I gave my face a quick wash in cold water and marched to Father's study. I tapped politely on the door.

'Come in.' Father looked up. 'Halloa Mary; what do you want? Have you quite recovered from seeing that villain?'

'I am quite recovered, Father, thank you.' I stepped into the room and perched myself, straight-backed, on the only other chair. 'It is that villain that I wish to ask you about.'

Father sipped at the glass of claret on his desk, shuffled his papers and looked at me. 'Ask away, Mary, although I do think you would be better employing your mind with thoughts of John Aitken.'

'John Aitken can whistle for all I care,' I said, rudely. 'No, father, it is that poor fellow you have in Muirend lockup I wish to ask you about.'

'So you said, Mary.' Father raised his eyebrows. 'What do you wish to know?'

'Are you sure he is a guilty party?' I was never known for my subtlety.

'At present, he is accused of many things,' Father looked directly at me, pressing his fingers onto the desk. 'His trial will determine if he is innocent or guilty.'

I had formulated my questions, but now I faced my father, my carefully crafted words flew out of the window. 'He looks too handsome to be guilty.' I knew that my words were foolish even as I said them.

'I am afraid that we cannot judge a man by his looks. I have known the most handsome men to be arrant rogues, and the ugliest men to have the hearts of saints and angels.'

'Surely you cannot keep the poor fellow locked up on the word of two known scoundrels,' I tried another approach.

'Would you prefer that I allowed a noted law-breaker to wander free, jeopardising the labours of innocent and hardworking people?' Father's voice was mild.

'He is not yet a noted law-breaker,' I said. 'You said the trial would determine his innocence or guilt.'

Father smiled. 'I wish that the law was open as a career to women, Mary, for by the powers, you would argue your case well. However, we have been searching for this fellow for some time.' He closed his hand into a fist. 'And now we have him, I intend to keep him fast until his trial.'

'Yes, Father.' I knew there any further argument would be pointless. That part of my plan had failed. I knew I must move onto my second stage. 'Thank you, Father. I am sure you are correct.'

I was not sure at all, of course, but I was determined to allay any suspicions Father may have about my future intentions.

I waited until midnight before making my move. In those days, we all went to bed early and arose before dawn. When I had been in Father's study, I saw a large key on his desk. That must be the key to the Muirend lockup. It could be no other. I dressed hurriedly, putting on my darkest, most close-fitting dress and sturdy boots. I envied men their freedom of movement with their breeches and trousers, but short of altering the order of the sexes, I could hardly don a male's clothing. The thought made me smile, although I did borrow one of father's old tricorne hats for this occasion.

I knew that Father kept his study locked, to ensure the security of his court documents. I also knew where he hung the key. It was the work of a moment to slide in, close the door behind me and search for the key to the lock-up. I had a moment of panic when I saw the surface of the desk was clear, and I spent some frantic seconds opening and closing Father's desk drawers until I found the key tucked under a wad of papers.

I left the study as I had found it, relocked the door, returned the door key to its hook and slipped downstairs. However well you know a place, there is always some obstacle in your path when you move in the dark. I must have stumbled over half the furniture in the house before I scraped open the bolts of our side door, wrestled with the lock and stepped into the dark. Fortunately, the night was dry and reasonably mild as I turned up the collar of my great cloak, pulled down father's tricorne hat and strode toward Muirend.

When I say strode, I should say felt my way gingerly, for the roads were un-made, rutted by cartwheels and generally treacherous. Those were the days before the transport improvements, with John Loudon McAdam still experimenting with his methods of road making in his Mauchline estate. I had brought a lantern but forbore to light it until I was well clear of the house. The last thing I wanted was for one of the servants to see a suspicious light flickering around the house. I could imagine the result, with Father and the footman coming out with pistols and cudgels, shots in the dark and me having a hundred unpleasant questions to answer.

Stumbling and falling, I left the grounds behind me, slid into the shelter of a copse of trees and scraped a spark from Father's tinderbox onto the wick of the lantern.

Shielding the light, I moved quickly toward Kirkton of Muirend. Twice I halted when I thought I heard somebody else moving around in the dark. Once it turned out to be a cow, strayed from its field. The second time I was not sure. An owl called eerily, joined by the harsh bark of a fox, which unsettled a shed full of hens that began to cackle in panic. I moved on.

Kirkton of Muirend was nothing special, a dozen cottages grouped around the ancient parish kirk, or church, with one stout building as the parish lock up. It was usually empty. When some unfortunate occupied the single cell, he or she would be there for drunkenness, poaching or affray. This time my unhappy Captain Ferintosh was inside on false charges made up by Peter and Simmy.

I halted outside the tiny window with its deeply set iron grill. There was no glass so the cold of the night could whistle inside to add to the discomfort of the occupant. 'Captain Ferintosh.' I whispered the name. There was no reply. I tried again. 'Captain Ferintosh!' Holding up the lantern, I peered inside the room but saw only shadows.

Fumbling for the key, I found the lock. It opened with surprising ease. I had thought it would be rusted.

'Captain Ferintosh?' I held the lantern high, with the light pooling inside the stark room. Stone walls above a stone-slabbed floor, with heavy wooden rafters beneath a roof of red pantiles, the cottage was no different from a thousand others in East Lothian except for the barred windows and the staples and chains on the wall.

'Who the devil is that?' Captain Ferintosh did not sound his usual cheerful self. 'Can't a man get a night's sleep without some blasted woman interrupting him?'

'It's me, Captain. It's Mary.' I held the lantern, so the light fell on my face.

'Lady Mary!' The tone of the captain's voice altered. 'What are you doing in a place like this?'

'Trying to rescue you,' I crouched at his side. 'You're chained up.'

'There's a key on that wall over there,' Captain Ferintosh nodded to the wall furthest from him.

It was the work of a moment to lift down the key and release the captain. He spent a moment rubbing his ankles and wrists, from which the manacles had rubbed the skin. 'You're an angel,' Captain Ferintosh said.

'My Father won't agree.'

'Come on, out of here,' Captain Ferintosh did not pursue that line of conversation. He limped to the door, gasping every time he put his left foot on the ground. I saw a dark stain in the middle of his thigh; blood from a wound, I guessed.

I replaced the key, relocked the door and stood outside the lockup. My plan had worked, but it had a serious flaw: I did not know what to do next. I had only thought as far as releasing the captain.

'You're free,' I said. 'I'll have to go home and put the key back, or Father will know it was me who got you out.'

There was an alternative. I could run away with the captain and share whatever adventures he had.

I contemplated that life for a moment, thinking of life on the high seas, or *on the pad* as we would-be-outlaws termed the bold roguery of the highwayman.

'Thank you.' Captain Ferintosh smiled, with those marvellous eyes dark and caring as he touched my face. 'Can I ask you one more favour?'

'Yes, of course.' I was genuinely pleased to help.

'Could you help me a little way from the village? I only have one working leg, you see.' Captain Ferintosh's smile was as winning as ever.

'What happened to your leg?'

'Your father shot me,' Captain Ferintosh showed no malice. Taking my hand in his, he lowered the lantern to enable me to see better. The blood-caked hole in his breeches told more than a hundred words could.

'Oh, you poor man!' I leant closer. 'We'll have to get you to a doctor.'

'I suspect that the minute I enter the premises of a sawbones, there will be a messenger running to your father.'

I could not disagree with that. Father knew all the local doctors.

'No, Miss Hepburn. If you help me to a friend of mine, he can patch me up most satisfactorily.'

'Come on then,' I loaned the captain my arm for support. 'Which way is it?'

'This way. It's a fair step, I'm afraid. A mile or two.'

I glanced at the overcast sky, wondering what time it was and if I could get home before dawn. I had no wish for Mother to discover my absence. However, as there was no help for it I buckled down, helped support the captain's weight and staggered along the rutted road. My lantern bounced its light around us, now showing the autumn-sad vegetation at the side of the path, now the bare trees above.

I cannot describe how it felt to be helping a man with whom I was in love. It was a mixture of pleasure that I was useful and trepidation that he might be seriously hurt. Add anxiety about my own situation and worry about the captain's future to the sauce and you will have some ideas about my feelings.

'Captain,' I said as we limped through the dark.

'Yes, Mary?'

'My father is convinced that you have committed some offence.' I waited for his reaction.

'I gathered that when he shot me.'

I took a deep breath. 'Have you committed an offence?'

Captain Ferintosh was silent for the next few yards. 'Would you have still helped me if I had?'

I thought for a moment. 'Yes, probably.'

The captain squeezed my arm. 'I thought you were game. In fact, I think you are the most game woman I have ever met.'

I am sure I glowed with pleasure.

'Leave me here.' The captain said. He had not answered my question. Perhaps he had forgotten. Maybe there was no need.

I looked around. 'There's nothing here,' I said. 'No house, not even a cottage.'

'That's all right,' the captain said. 'I know where I am.'

We were in an area of unenclosed land, with a range of miniature hills, the Garleton Hills, rising before us. Beyond that, the ground fell away to the coastal plain. My captain was limping heavily. Only the night-dark Huntlaw House, home of the eccentric Lady Emily, sat in a neuk of the hills to the north.

'I can't leave you here,' I said.

'Leave me,' Captain Ferintosh had a new edge to his voice. 'I know where I am.'

'Will you be all right?' I asked. 'When will I see you again?'

His eyes seemed to glow in the dark. 'I'll contact you. Now go.' He pushed me gently. 'Go, Mary.'

'I can't leave you like this,' I said. 'I love you.'

There. I had said it. The words were out. I had committed myself. There was no going back.

'Good God!' Captain Ferintosh stared at me. 'You know, I really think you do. Well now, my poor, sweet little girl.'

'Captain,' I held out my hands to him. 'I can't leave you here. It's not safe for you.'

'Go,' he said. 'You must go.'

'But, Captain…'

'But me no buts.' He pushed me again, gently but firmly. 'Go now, Lady Mary. You can do no more.'

I hated to leave him there all alone, wounded in the dark. I took one step and looked back over my shoulder. He had not moved. He waved me away. I took another step.

I heard movement in the dark. 'Captain Ferintosh,' I said.

He was gone. I did not see him move. One moment he was there, the next I was alone in the chilly emptiness.

Loneliness is a strange concept. Normally I enjoy my own company best as many people are irritating with their pettiness and only desire to be the same as everybody else. However, there are times that I seek out the warmth and essential congeniality of people, for beneath the façade of bland acceptability most are decent. When I realised that I was alone on that barren track beside these great grassy lumps of hills, I suddenly felt very lonely.

I did not linger long. After a few moments in which I stared into the night, I turned and strode purposefully in the direction of home. I knew I had a few miles to cover, it was late, I was tired, and somehow I had to replace the key in father's desk and later explain how I managed to get mud on my skirt while sleeping in bed.

I did not expect to see the man who loomed out of the dark.

'Where are you going all alone, my pretty?'

'Who are you?' I demanded, more irritated than afraid. 'Get out of my way!'

'What have we here?' The voice sounded again. 'It's a woman!'

The light shone full in my face and a pair of strong arms fastened around me.

I gasped, with horrible memories of Simmy and Peter coming back to me. 'Let go,' I said. I am not sure what happened next. There was a shout, somebody hit the man who held me and dragged me away.

'Stay with me.' A man's voice hissed in my ear.

'Why? Who...?' I got no further in my enquiries as a hand clamped across my mouth. Honestly, the number of times I was manhandled that autumn!

Pulled backwards, I was led into the darkest section of a field and forced down. For a moment I contemplated the worst type of horrors imaginable.

'If I take my hand away, will you promise to keep quiet?'

I nodded vigorously, although I had every intention of screaming the countryside awake if this man did not behave himself.

'Brave girl.' The hand slipped away as the man whispered. 'Now lie still until it's safe.'

'What's happening?' I forgot my promise immediately.

'Sssh!' The hand hovered near my mouth again.

I shushed. I lay on the chill grass with this strange man beside me. I heard gruff voices echoing through the dark, somebody coughed and swore obscenely. The wind carried the words away. The man beside me shifted.

'Wait here,' the man touched my arm. 'Don't move until I return.'

He was gone. I lay alone, not sure what I should do. This night was not going as I had intended. Was it always like this at night, beyond the confines of Cauldneb? No wonder Mother had always insisted that I stayed inside our policies when the darkness crept in.

'We're safe,' I had not heard the man return. 'Follow me. Don't stray.' I saw the flash of teeth as he smiled. 'Take hold of my coat tails.'

I did as he said, still not sure what was happening as we trailed across the fields, avoiding the roads. Twice we stopped while my anonymous escort checked ahead.

'Here we are.' The man stopped at the gateway to our policies. 'I'll leave you here.'

'Who are you?' I tried to peer through the dark. 'How do you know where I live?' The man stepped back. The breeze pushed the clouds clear of the scimitar moon. For a moment I had a clear view of my companion's features. Even so, I was little further forward for he had taken the precaution of blackening his face. He looked more like a collier than anything else. Only his eyes were clear; they must have been the steadiest I had ever seen.

'Who are you?' I repeated, but I was talking to empty air. My steady-eyed companion had vanished in the night.

I had left the side door open so returning into the house was easy. The long-case clock in the lobby said a quarter before four. I had been out of the house for less than four hours; it seemed like days. Waves of tiredness swept over me as I crept upstairs to Father's study. Replacing the key, I threw off my clothes and fell into bed without bothering to don my night things. My mind was in a state of confusion mixed with vague guilt.

Had I done the right thing in freeing Captain Ferintosh? Who were the men who had tried to grab me? Most of all, who was the steady-eyed man who had guided me home? Would Mother notice the mud on my cloak or could I claim it was from my last walk on Lammermuir?

Even with my brain in a whirl, I slept like a felled log. Mother had to call me several times next morning before she sent up Maggie, our newest maid to wake me.

'Oh, Miss,' Maggie giggled to find me *au naturel.* 'You are all naked.'

'So are you, under your clothes.' I am not at my best in the morning after only two hours sleep. I threw on the first things that came to hand, shoved my cloak at poor Maggie with orders to get it cleaned and stomped downstairs in a foul mood. I soon realised that my perfect pater was in a temper equally as ferocious as my own. I had often wondered from whom I had inherited my disposition.

Chapter Seven

'Escaped?' I heard father's voice from two rooms away. 'How the devil did he escape? He was under lock and key and chained to the wall for God's sake.'

I kept quiet as I sneaked into the dining room. Mother glowered at me for being late, while shaking her head as a warning not to interrupt Father at his rantings.

'Somebody must have broken him out,' Elliot and Flockhart had brought Father the news.

'Let me see.' Father did not bother to pull on a coat as he dashed out of the house. 'Fetch Hector! At once, do you hear?'

You can only guess how I felt when I saw the consternation creasing Father's face. He was a good man holding his family together while trying to preserve the peace, and here I had increased his troubles. My heart sunk as I watched Father mount Hector and nearly gallop from the policies.

What had I done?

'Are you all right, Miss Mary?' Jeannie, the housekeeper, had known me all my life. 'Don't you fret about your father. He knows what's what.'

'Yes.' I guessed how false my smile must have been. 'Yes, I'm sure he does.'

'I'm sure your mother will find you something to keep your mind off things.' Jeannie said, kindly. 'You go and find her, now.'

'Yes.' I stood up. The last person I wanted to see was my mother. I could not face her, knowing what I had done. 'I can't stay in the house. I have to go outside.'

'I'll tell your mother,' Jeannie said. 'I know how you don't like to be cooped up indoors.'

Only pausing to thank Jeannie, I slipped on my boots and cloak. I had too much on my mind to stay indoors. Fortunately, Coffee was rested, and in her stable, so I helped the stable lad saddle her and fled Cauldneb.

I rode blindly, allowing Coffee to pick the road as the wind soothed my guilt and ruffled my hair. I had jammed Father's old hat on my head again, as much for convenience as anything else. Now I pulled it further down and headed north, toward the coast, or toward the Garleton Hills. The first frost of the season nipped my face, freezing the tears on my cheeks, but also kept my mind active as I pondered my actions.

I came to myself when I saw the old-fashioned coach lumber across the appallingly rutted roads of the Huntlaw Estate.

Everybody knew that Lady Emily Hume of Huntlaw was eccentric. She would emerge from Huntlaw House at odd times of the day or night, ride around the countryside and return without anybody seeing her face or speaking to her. Her chariot lurched past me as I walked Coffee on the fringes of her land. I lifted a hand to acknowledge her coachman's waved greeting. He looked even older than the coach.

I reined up nearly at the same spot I had left Captain Ferintosh the previous night. Already it seemed a long time ago. I looked around, wondering how the captain had vanished so completely and where he might be now. How much had happened in such a short space of time with that strange man coming to my aid.

Lady Emily's chariot disappeared behind a new plantation as I walked Coffee around the borders of the recently ploughed field.

The man and I saw each other simultaneously. I frowned, recognising Alexander Colligere. I raised my hand, glad to see a face that might prove to be friendly.

Alexander marched across to me, with a large canvas bag in one hand and a small trowel in the other. 'Good day Miss Hepburn.' He shouted across to me. 'What brings you here?'

'I'm just out for a ride,' I could hardly say that I was looking for a prisoner I had helped escape. I nodded to the bag. 'That looks interesting.'

'Oh,' Alexander's smile could not have been broader. 'I'm collecting samples, you see.' He held the bag open for my inspection. 'One never knows what one can find, especially in fields that have been neglected, or down by the coast where ships call from foreign parts.'

'Samples?' I peered into the bag. Mr Ormiston had been correct, Alexander was a little touched; his bag was full of the sort of weeds that I routinely plucked from our garden and threw into Mr Mitchell's fire.

'Plant samples,' Alexander said. 'I collect and label them.' He told me the Latin names, pointing out each one.

'Why do you do that?' I temporarily forgot my mission as I tried to fathom this man. I had never met a man who collected weeds.

'They are fascinating things.' Alexander sounded genuinely enthusiastic about the green jumble inside his bag. 'Why are you here? Is it something to do with that excitement last night?'

I had not expected anybody to make that connection. 'What makes you ask that?' I wished this strange man would go and grub for his weeds and leave me in peace to search for Captain Ferintosh.

'One of the servants mentioned there had been noises around here last night,' Alexander said, 'and you don't normally come this way.'

'How do you know that?' I demanded abruptly. 'Have you been spying on me?'

'Good heavens, no!' Alexander smiled at the idea. 'I saw you for the first time yesterday, Miss Hepburn. No, I've been searching for plants in this area every day for the past week, and nobody has come except Lady Emily in her coach.'

'Oh,' I immediately regretted my outburst. 'I'm sorry, Mr Colligere.'

Alexander's smile dropped. 'Oh, please don't apologise to me. It was an easy assumption. I should have made myself clearer.'

Alexander's words made me feel worse, of course. I tried to make amends and succeeded in making things worse. 'What will you do with all your weeds?' *Plants! They are plants!*

'They're not weeds,' Alexander defended his collection. 'Or rather I don't consider them as weeds, whatever others may think.'

'What will you do with your plants?' I amended, wishing I had never started this conversation. *Would this man not go away and allow me to look for Captain Ferintosh?*

Alexander grinned, evidently pleased that I was taking an interest in his eccentricity. 'I am storing and cataloguing them,' he said. 'I aim to find all the native plants first, and then see the incomers, those that have arrived here from foreign parts.'

I found that strangely interesting. 'Why?'

'To see what can grow best in this soil,' Alexander's enthusiasm was obvious. 'We are in a period of tremendous advancement,' he said. 'Our agricultural techniques are advancing year on year, so why not our horticulture and botany as well? We have little idea what good can come from plants, medicine as well as food. My mother was a healer; she knew what plants healed sicknesses.'

I had no desire to hear about this man's mother, for goodness sake. 'Father is always trying to improve our farms,' I said.

'Is he?' I had never seen a man so animated about farming as Alexander Colligere was when I mentioned Father's agricultural engagement. His whole face seemed to become alive in a most curious manner. 'I shall have to talk to him, I am sure we have much to discuss.'

'I'm sure you would both enjoy that,' I said, resolving to stay well away from the meeting. 'You may wish to speak to Mr Mitchell our gardener too.'

Alexander did not seem to realise I had insulted him by putting him on the same social level as a servant. *Why had I done that? That was the sort of statement my mother would have made when she put somebody in their place.*

'I'm sure we will have a great deal in common,' Alexander was as enthusiastic as if I had proposed a hunt or a ball. I had never met such a man before.

'Well, Mr Colligere,' I said, 'I will be on my way. Good luck with your plant hunting.' Tapping Coffee with the reins, I pulled past him and walked on, not quite sure where I was going.

'My name is not...' I had heard enough of Alexander's words to listen to any more.

Lady Emily's coach passed on her return home. It halted, and for a long moment, I saw the white blur of a face at the side window. Either Her Ladyship was watching me ride around her lands, or she was wondering what Alexander Colligere was doing hacking at her weeds. I shook my head: two eccentrics on the same patch of land; they were well suited to one another.

It was not until I passed the Garleton Hills that I realised there had been no formality between us. I had spoken to Alexander as if I had known him for years. I shook away that thought. It was far more important that I find Captain Ferintosh.

I found that Father had the same concern when I returned after a long and fruitless ride. My mood, you may guess, was none the sweeter for my failure.

'He has vanished like smoke on a windy day.' Father fumed as he dismounted in front of our stables. 'I have alerted the parish constables all over the county, sent intelligence to all the magistrates and ordered his description to be published in the newspapers.' He stamped his feet in frustration. 'I am deeply embarrassed at having such a prize escape from my custody!'

I said nothing although my guilt must have been evident in my flushed face and averted gaze. I was about to retreat to my room when a whole press of riders clattered into our courtyard, with the sound of the horses' hooves ringing on the cobble-stones and the sight and smell of the beasts reminding me of the olden days of cattle reiving and English invasion.

'Damn the man!' Mr John Aitken shouted. 'Damn and blast him for an errant rogue.'

I listened. As Father was not prone to such colourful language, it was quite entertaining to hear a man carry on so.

'How the deuce did he escape?' Mr Aitken asked when he calmed down.

'There was no sign of forced entry at the lockup,' Father said. 'He must have a cracksman in his gang, some expert from Edinburgh to pick the lock.' He clenched his single fist. 'I'd like to get my hand on the fellow that released him!'

'What has he done to have a gang?' I thought it best to change the subject before Father began to ask about keys. 'Who is this fellow that caused you so much distress?'

'You saw him yesterday, Miss Hepburn,' Mr Aitken said. 'He is the most roguish blackguard in Scotland, fit to match any outlaw, by God.'

'Pray, sir,' I approached, promising myself that whatever happened, I would not marry this foul-mouthed, blustering old man. 'Does he have a name?' I hoped that they had arrested the wrong fellow, you understand. I hoped that my gallant captain was as innocent of crime as I had been this time yesterday.

'He has a name indeed,' Blustering John Aitken said. 'He has a name for rascally and impertinence, for illicit distilling; he has a name for roguery and deception, for lies and blackguardism; he has a name for theft and smuggling and even murder I wouldn't wonder. In short, Miss Hepburn, he is a scoundrel of the highest order, a man who deserves a good hanging.'

'Yes, Mr Aitken,' I thought it politic to agree to John Aitken's assassination of my good captain's character. 'But does he have a given name? Is he Mr Smith for instance? Or is he Angus MacDonald? Or perhaps he is Edward Largelugs?'

John Aitken's glare should have consigned me to the deepest pit, which was possibly the intention of that choleric gentleman. 'He has many given names as well, Miss Hepburn. Unfortunately, we do not know which one is correct. Some call him Edmund Charleton. Others know him as Galloping Bob. The ladies, I hear, call him Captain Ferintosh.'

I knew that last name.

'Oh.' It was true then. Father had not mistakenly arrested the wrong man. My oh-so-gallant captain was a black-hearted villain, by the sound of it, a criminal of the highest order. I took a deep breath, remembering Captain Ferintosh's kindness to me. 'He can't be all bad,' I said. 'There will be some good in him.'

Father put his arm around me. 'That is typical of my daughter, John. Mary looks for the good in everybody. You will learn to love her as much as we do.'

The idea of grumpy John Aitken loving me was more than I could bear. The thought of his huge, calloused hands on my body... No! I refused to even contemplate such a thing.

'There is no good in Edmund Charleton,' John Aitken said. 'He is dyed black as the Earl of Hell's weskit.'

I compared Captain Ferintosh's elegant manners with John Aitken's foul temper. I knew which gentleman I preferred. I did not care what misdemeanours John Aitken accused Captain Ferintosh of. The captain had always been a perfect gentleman with me.

'Father mentioned a gang,' I reminded. 'Do you know what sort of gang, pray?'

'A gang of the worst kind of wicked blaggards imaginable,' John Aitken said. 'It is a gang of thieves and cutpurses, cracksmen and smugglers. Why his very name gives away the kind of men who would be attracted to him!'

'Edmund Charleton,' I said. 'That does not sound too bad to me.'

'Galloping Bob or Captain Ferintosh,' John Aitken said.

Father watched, saying nothing. I presumed that he was allowing John Aitken and I to get acquainted. *Well, Father,* I thought, *I have had all the acquaintance I wish with this fellow.*

'Galloping Bob,' I said. 'That sounds romantic.'

'It is a fine name for a highwayman,' John Aitken grumbled.

I agreed. A highwayman, the knights of the road, would be proud of that name. I wondered if my captain had ever been such a gallant, taking his life in his hands, robbing the rich to protect the poor.

'Captain Ferintosh as well.' I rolled the name around inside my head. 'It sounds Highland, like one of the chiefs who raised these regiments to fight the French in the last war. Ferintosh's Highlanders. It's a name fit to stand beside Fraser's Highlanders who captured Quebec, or Montgomery's Highlanders that fought in the West Indies and against the ferocious Shawnee warriors.'

I was teasing, of course, showing grumpy John Aitken that I was not impressed by his attack on the escaped prisoner.

'It is Highland,' Father did not sound pleased. 'Ferintosh is another name for whisky, particularly smuggled whisky. This fellow, Charleton or Galloping whatever, pretends to be a gallant captain when in reality he is the leader of one of the most notorious illicit whisky distilling bands I have ever come across.' Father faced me squarely. 'John is correct in all he says, Mary. Charleton is a despicable rogue. I hope we can recapture him before he causes any more mayhem.'

Father's words removed any trace of levity from me. I had never known him so serious when talking to me. Unable to meet his eyes, I looked away. 'Yes, Father.' Once again I regretted my impulsive actions. I should have let Captain Ferintosh prove his innocence in the court rather than distress my father in this manner.

I was twenty years old, a young woman rather than a girl, yet I had acted like an irresponsible child. Retreating to the walled garden, I sought solace among the plants and sounds of nature. I had lived a comparatively sheltered life, I admit, but I was no fool. I should not have gone against my father, who always acted with fairness and impartiality. He tempered justice with mercy, veering toward leniency in more cases than he would admit himself.

Why had I acted as I had? Love of course. I had fallen in love with Captain Ferintosh. I still loved him, despite all I had heard. Father and John Aitken must be mistaken. I nodded as I walked between the neat vegetable beds. That was the only answer. Father had made an honest mistake.

What if Father was right?

I could not believe that. I could not allow myself to think that I had released such an evil man. I was quite prepared to accept that Captain Ferintosh was a bit of a rogue, in the stamp of Rob Roy MacGregor or one of the old Border Reivers, a laughing, gallant daredevil who danced on the borders of legitimacy, but I refused to believe that he was an out-and-out villain.

Ignoring the rain that had oozed from a leaden sky, I continued to pace between the vegetable beds and fruit bushes. Somewhere in my mind, I hoped that Captain Ferintosh would pop up behind me, as he had before. That miracle did not happen. Captain Ferintosh did not come. Instead, it Mr Mitchell arrived, pushing the inevitable wheelbarrow.

'You had better get yourself inside out of the rain, Miss Mary.' He had watched me grow up and knew me as well as he knew his own children. 'You'll get into bother with your mother else.'

'Thank you, Mr Mitchell.' I had called him Mr since my infancy. 'I'll just stay out here. I like to think.'

'Whatever you think best, Miss Mary.' Mr Mitchell disappeared into the potting shed, his personal haven where he smoked his pipe, sipped at his illicit whisky that I pretended to know nothing about, and worked his wizardry on the plants.

Alone once more, my mind reverted to the problem of Captain Ferintosh. I could think of only one solution: seek him out and persuade him to return to Father's custody.

To me, that seemed the best way for everybody. Father would have his prisoner back, so would retain his reputation as a safe pair of hands while Captain Ferintosh would help his case by returning voluntarily, and would have the opportunity to clear his name. Most of all, I would lose the guilt that hung like a lead weight around my heart. Once the captain was released and free of any accusation, I could openly declare my affection for him. John Aitken could pack his feelings for me in a small sack and bury them wherever he felt best, for I did not, and could not care a flying fig for him or a hundred more John Aitkens however worthy they may be.

I sighed, looking up into the refreshing rain. God was in his heaven, and all was bright in the world. All I had to do was turn my theory into practice.

'Mary!' My mother's carping voice rang through the garden. 'You'll catch your death of fever. I don't want the expense of burying you, next!'

'Yes, Mother,' I obeyed like the dutiful daughter that I was. I knew what I wanted to do. I was determined to right my wrong.

Chapter Eight

I sat at the breakfast table as Father entertained Mr Ormiston, John Aitken and the hard-eyed Mr Elliot. Mother sat opposite Father as the men demolished all the food Cook could provide.

Once the initial grumbling about the state of farming and the price of grain had been disposed of, Mother steered the conversation away from Captain Ferintosh's mysterious escape to her favourite subject.

'You are a married man, are you not, Mr Ormiston?'

'I am, Mrs Hepburn.' Mr Ormiston did not strike me as the marrying type. I thought him sarcastic, unpleasant and nasty.

'Do you have any family, Mr Ormiston?'

'I have two sons and one daughter,' Ormiston said. I pitied these little ones under his sneering eye.

'Mrs Ormiston will be busy with all these children to bring up.' Mother looked sideways at me, doubtless ensuring I was taking notes of how a dutiful wife should act.

'Poor Hannah works non-stop,' Mr Ormiston said. 'We have employed a nanny to help her.'

I nodded to him, grudgingly seeing some good in this sardonic man. 'Mrs Ormiston will be grateful for that.'

'The two of them get along famously,' Ormiston said. 'I've never seen such a pair for laughing together.' Ormiston's eyes altered amazingly when he spoke of his wife. They sparkled with deep affection. I thought I might actually like the man.

'I am glad to hear that,' Mother said. She turned her attention to Mr Elliot. 'How is Mrs Elliot?'

'In charge of everything,' Elliot replied at once. 'People who think that men are the head of the house have evidently never met Mrs Elliot.'

I hid my smile. Mr Elliot was one of the most direct men I had ever met. I could not imagine him taking orders from a woman.

'I like the sound of her,' Mother glanced at Father, who, thinking I was not looking, pulled a face.

'Mr Aitken.' At last, Mother came to the real object of her attention. I knew her methods, you see. She had been trying to allay my suspicions by asking all the men present about their wives while waiting to pounce on John Aitken. 'You are without a wife at present, I understand.'

'You understand correctly, Mrs Hepburn.' Was that a meaningful glance at me? Or was I imagining things? I was sure it was a meaningful glance. I quailed; the formal before-declaration-of-marriage-intent-meeting was meant to be on Saturday week, not today.

Deciding to say nothing, I clamped shut my mouth and stared fixedly at the picture on the wall as if I had never before seen the landscape of the Forth.

'I am sure you miss your dear departed Mrs Aitken.' Mother nearly purred the words.

'I am sure I do not,' John Aitken spoke with some heat. 'She was an old witch. She would put a spell on me like as not, the instant I decided to do anything that met with her disapproval.'

I smiled, thinking that John Aitken was making a joke.

'It was no laughing matter, Miss Hepburn,' Grumpy John Aitken snapped. 'I was glad when she decided to die on me. I buried her face-downward so if she tried to crawl out of her grave she will be ever closer to where she belongs.'

I had a mental image of poor Mrs Aitken exiting through the floor of her coffin and scrabbling down, down, down in the hope of haunting her husband. I did not smile; in my mind, John and Mrs Aitken seemed well suited for each other.

'I believe that you are searching for another wife?' Mother spoke artlessly as if she had not been leading up to that question since we first sat at the table.

I felt John Aitken's eyes swivel to me and away again. 'I will be very careful before I commit myself to another marriage.' He spoke slowly. 'I wish for a wife with an even temper next time around.'

I said nothing, wondering how I could unleash my wicked temper without further upsetting my father.

'I'm sure you will find the right lady,' Mother spoke soothingly. She looked across at me. 'Every man needs a good wife to look after him.'

As I prepared to show my temper, Ormiston forestalled me. 'I was saying that to Colligere this morning. A good wife is what you need, I said. Take Mrs Ormiston now, a better wife you could not find.'

I wondered what Alexander Colligere would do with a wife. He would probably label her and place her in a box with his other exhibits. 'Mrs Colligere would have to be a very understanding woman,' I said.

Ormiston laughed. 'She need not worry about any love rival,' he said. 'Her only jealousy would be reserved for a new type of grass, or weed, or potato, perhaps.'

We smiled at each other in perfect understanding. I had thought that Ormiston had been cruel with his description of Mr Colligere, now I understood the affection peeping from behind the words. Rather than an unpleasant, unfeeling fellow, Ormiston hid his kindness by a mask of barbed words.

The rap at the door interrupted our meal. The footman poked his head into the room. 'My apologies for interrupting, Mr Hepburn, but there is a message for you.' He proffered a silver tray on which lay a folded piece of paper, sealed with a wafer.

Father broke the seal and read the note. 'I am sorry, gentlemen. My apologies, Agnes, I am afraid I must break up this happy gathering.'

Mother nodded at once. 'I understand, Andrew. What has occurred, pray?'

'The Revenue cutter has caught a Dutch smuggler off Dunbar.' Father said.

I could not hide my relief. I had been concerned that Captain Ferintosh might have been involved.

'I must repair to the courthouse at Haddington,' Father said. 'There is some legal wrangle they wish to clear up.'

'You other gentlemen are welcome to stay,' Mother said.

'It would not be right,' Mr Ormiston said. 'We must bid you farewell, Mrs Hepburn.'

'Gentlemen,' Mother gave a broad smile. 'I would deem it a great favour if you would stay a little longer. An hour or two, while Mr Hepburn is away. I am a little unsettled with these unpleasant rogues around.'

I looked at mother, aware that she was as unsettled as a lump of granite on a still day. That woman was planning something.

The men glanced at each other.

'Only one gentleman will suffice,' Mother said. 'Mr Ormiston and Mr Elliot; you had better return to your wives. They will be as troubled as I am. I do apologise, Mr Aitken for the inconvenience.'

I was surprised when Mr Aitken gave a polite bow. 'There is no inconvenience, Mrs Hepburn. I am honoured to be of assistance.' He exchanged glances with Father. 'I will ride to Tyneford first, with your permission. I must ensure my men are working.'

'Thank you, Mr Aitken.' Mother said. 'I am most grateful.'

When Father rose, the room cleared in seconds, leaving Mother and I staring at each other across the desolate table.

'That was rather sudden,' Mother said. 'I am glad it is only a legal matter this time.'

'So am I.' I said. 'I didn't like it at all when Father rode out with his pistol. It's like the old days of the Border Wars.'

'I agree.' Mother sat back in her chair. 'Who is this Mr Colligere fellow that you and Mr Ormiston were discussing?'

'Mr Colligere,' the thought of Alexander Colligere made me smile. 'He is the gentleman who ended up on the floor with Mr Aitken.'

'I remember Mr Aitken falling,' Mother said. 'I cannot for the life of me recall who else was involved. No matter.' Mother shook her head. 'You heard me ask Mr John Aitken to keep us company for a while.'

'Yes, Mother.' I said. 'I do not understand why.'

'You will,' Mother was smiling. 'I'm too busy, so this is a good time for you to get to know him better.'

'Mother!' I stared at her in horror. I honestly felt sick at the thought of even being near the man. I also knew that mother was only making an excuse to push me and John Aitken together.

'I want you to play the hostess,' Mother continued as if I had consented without demur.

'I'd rather not,' I said.

'I know you'd rather not,' Mother's smile did not falter. 'But I would rather that you did.'

That ended the discussion of course. In my day, it was a foolish woman indeed who dared deny her mother's wishes. I spent the next hour or two waiting in increasing trepidation for Mr Aitken to return. I could not leave the house so fretted at my sewing, pricking my finger more than once. Eventually we heard a knock at the front door.

Mother looked up with a smile. 'Get the poor fellow a drink, Mary. Show him around the house. Show him the grounds too, if time permits.'

'You would be far better at that than I, Mother,' I searched for a way out.

'Oh, don't be silly, Mary.' Mother picked up a closed fan to tap me on the head. 'Just be yourself. Don't let your nerves get the better of you; if I am correct, Mr John Aitken will be family soon.' She leaned closer to me. 'I am always correct, Mary Agnes Hepburn, always correct.' She rapped my somewhat prominent rump with her fan, hard enough to make me jump. 'Now get along with you.' Mother always treated me as if I were ten years old, rather than as a woman fast approaching twenty-one.

With no choice in the matter, I was not sure whether to deliberately spoil the occasion for Mr Aitken, or impress him. In the event, I decided to take Mother's advice and just be myself. After all, that was the easiest option.

John Aitken looked surprised when I greeted him in the withdrawing room. 'Good morning again, Miss Hepburn.' He gave a formal bow.

'Good morning Mr Aitken,' I curtseyed in return. 'I'm afraid Mother is indisposed at present. She asked if I could look after you.'

'How very thoughtful of her,' John Aitken said.

'Do you wish a drink, Mr Aitken?'

'Claret if I may,' Mr Aitken said. 'Will you be joining me? I always feel guilty when the ladies do without.'

That surprised me. Only a couple of hours previously I had thought this man to be a bit of a boor yet here he was displaying manners and consideration for others. 'I shall also have some claret.' Rather than ring for a servant, I poured two glasses myself.

'You have a generous hand,' Mr Aitken lifted his glass. 'May I propose a toast, Miss Hepburn? A happy future.'

'A happy future,' I repeated. *But not with you.*

'Mother suggested that I show you around Cauldneb' I said.

'That was very also thoughtful of her,' Mr Aitken said. 'Lead on MacDuff.'

So MacDuff led on. Mr Aitken must have been determined to make a good impression on me, for he smiled at my weak attempts at humour, reacted with politeness to my bald statements and tried to appear interested in everything I showed him.

Rather than the embarrassing time I had anticipated, I found myself quite liking this side of Mr Aitken, despite my wishes to the contrary.

Mr Aitken listened intently when I gave him a tour of the library. He examined the books I singled out and commented on the number of travel and botanical volumes we had. 'Your father must be interested in such things.'

'My father's interests lie chiefly in agriculture,' I said. 'These are books he purchased specifically for me.'

'Oh?' Mr Aitken's bushy eyebrows rose. 'It is unusual to find a young woman with such singular tastes.'

'You may find that not all young women come out of the same box, sir.' I felt my temper rising. Well then, let him see what manner of tartar he would get if he married me.

I had anticipated a warm response. I was surprised when Mr Aitken merely smiled. 'Very droll, Miss Hepburn. Very droll. I do like a woman with a sense of wit. My wife had no such pleasant attributes.'

Mr Aitken strolled to the window. 'You have rather a splendid vista from here.'

'Yes, Mr Aitken.' My temper cooled as rapidly as it had arisen. 'We can see most of the East Lothian plain.'

'That house there.' He pointed with the now-empty glass he still carried. 'I do not think I have noticed it before.'

'No, Mr Aitken,' I said. 'That is the roof and bell tower of Huntlaw House. It hides in the folds of the Garleton Hills.'

'Ah, Huntlaw.' Mr Aitken nodded. 'I believe I have heard the name. Was there not some tragedy attached to it?'

'Why yes,' I said. 'Many years ago Lord Hume of Huntlaw died in a hunting accident. He was out shooting wildfowl in Aberlady Bay when his son accidentally shot him. Poor Lord Hume was killed outright. Lady Hume was quite distraught.'

'I can imagine that she was,' Mr Aitken said. 'What happened to the son?'

'Alas, Mr Aitken, nobody knows. The story goes that he ran away, overcome with grief at what he had done. Poor Lady Hume has become a virtual recluse since then. She only leaves Huntlaw House a few times each week, when she sits in her coach to be driven around her lands, searching for her missing son.'

'What an unfortunate sequence of events.' Mr Aitken stared toward Huntlaw House. 'What a terrible tragedy for Lady Emily to lose both her husband and her son in such a manner.'

'Yes.' I patted Mr Aitken's shoulder. The poor old fellow seemed as troubled as Lady Emily had been.

Mr Aitken took hold of my hand. 'You have a kind heart, Miss Hepburn.' He smiled and released me. 'You will make a fine wife and mother.'

I avoided that subject.

'Is that your famous walled garden down there?' Mr Aitken asked.

'It is my favourite place in the world,' I said, 'save perhaps for the uplands of Lammermuir.'

'Your father has told me about your love for gardening.' Mr Aitken gave another small smile. 'It often got you into trouble with Mrs Hepburn.'

'When I was younger,' I said quickly, colouring. I hoped Father had not gone into too much detail about these long-gone incidents.

Mr Aitken softened his voice. 'Such things happened to us all.' He leaned closer to me. 'Very often to me when I was young.'

I nodded, surprised that he understood. I could see Mr Aitken in an entirely different light now. He was no ogre, as I had imagined. Rather, he seemed to be a sympathetic sort of man. I hated to admit to myself that I had developed a tolerance for Mr Aitken, perhaps even a faint liking.

Mother, naturally, saw all and understood everything. I am sure there was something of the witch about that woman.

'I thought the two of you would get along well enough,' Mother said later when Father claimed Mr Aitken for some business matter.

'Well enough,' I agreed, cautiously.

'That is good for both of you.' Mother tapped me with her closed fan once more. 'Any discord within a family leads to a miserable existence for everybody. I won't hear of my daughter being the source of any disharmony.' She strode away, no doubt satisfied that her plans for my wedding were progressing satisfactorily.

Chapter Nine

Two days later, I again left the house. With Father at the courthouse in Haddington and Mother talking to Cook in the kitchen, I left Coffee in the stable and walked to the Garleton Hills. Once again I had discarded everything but the most practical of clothing, with a warm skirt of autumn brown, stout boots for the muddy fields, a travelling cloak of the same hue and my father's oldest tricorne hat. I was growing rather fond of that battered old hat.

'Where are you off to, Mary?'

'I'm off for a walk, Mother.' I said. 'I might call in at Catherine Brown.' I wondered if I could take Catherine into my confidence over all that had happened but decided that the temptation to say too much would be too great for even Catherine to bear.

It is a weary step from Cauldneb to the Garleton Hills, so I was ready for a seat long before I arrived. The rain of the previous evening had cleared, leaving one of those crisp, bright days that make living in East Lothian such a delight. I perched myself on a recently erected drystane dyke, munched the bread and cheese that Cook had provided and wondered what to do next.

I knew what I wished to do, and that was to find Captain Ferintosh and persuade him to give himself up to Father. However, there is many a slip twixt the cup and the lip, as the old saying goes. My lip was my intention, with my cup being the actuality. I sat on that dyke for some time with the coldness of the stones gradually working its way into my rather ample nether portions. I had a splendid view of the hills from my position. They were not tall hills by Scottish standards, but in the plain of East Lothian they rose into quite a significant landmark.

Dressed in brown and with my back to the trunk of a weather-twisted old tree, I must have been nearly invisible to any casual traveller. I saw Lady Emily's coach trundle past without stopping. I saw a kestrel out hunting and heard the screaming of a hundred seagulls as they followed the plough in a field downhill and closer to the sea. I did not see the man until he appeared from nowhere.

For a moment I wondered if he were the mysterious man who had guided me through the dark a few nights ago, but somehow I knew that he was not. Even with my mind full of Captain Ferintosh and John Aitken, I had thought about that strong, confident figure that had appeared at just the right moment. *Who had he been?*

The man seemed to have risen from the middle of the hill. If I was ten rather than twenty, I might have thought he had emerged from fairyland. As it was, I remained still, with the final crust of my lunch held in my hand. I watched the man walk somewhat furtively across the field, vault over a dry-stane dyke at right angles to my own and part-stride, part-trot along the road to Haddington.

Now, where did you come from? I repeated the words in my head. *You must have come from somewhere; you could not spring from the earth, although you seemed to do just that.*

Naturally, I had to go and investigate. The time was passing, with the bright morning having turned into a blustery afternoon where a north-easterly wind threw squalls of near-sleet onto my face. Head down, I hurried across the field and onto the slippery grass slope of Craigie Hill, where I had first seen the man. Of course, he could have been entirely innocent, a farm servant on some errand, a man off to Haddington to purchase a gift for his sweetheart, or a labouring man returning home. However, given my previous history in this area, I doubted the innocence of anything or anybody here.

I had not been aware of the existence of the ruined castle at the foot of the hill, with its tumbledown walls, gun-loops and large chambers. On any other occasion, I would have spent time exploring the ruins. Today I only checked to see if my man could have emerged from within the massive walls. He could not. He came from further up the slope, so, hitching up my skirt to protect it from the wet grass, I set myself to climb.

Compared to Lammermuir, Craigie Hill was nothing. I was at the top within a few moments, with an immense panorama stretching around me.

'Halloa again.'

The voice was familiar but distorted. I looked around. 'Who said that?'

'Why, I did.'

'Who are you?' I could see nobody. 'Come out, sir, and stop skulking like a Frenchman!'

'Do the French skulk? I thought they were a formidably brave set of fellows when I met them.'

'Who are you, sir?' I looked behind me. Nobody. I looked to each side; only the empty hillside of grass and the occasional rocky outcrop stretching to the level plain beneath.

'It's me, Mary; it's Alexander.'

'Alexander Colligere? Are you here again?' I sighed. That man had obviously been sent by a vengeful God to plague me because of my sin in releasing Captain Ferintosh from durance vile. 'Where are you, sir? Show yourself, I demand it!' There was my temper revealing itself, you see. If only I could have been that open with John Aitken, I would have scared him off to find a woman more his own age.

'Here I am.' Alexander appeared before me, grinning like an overgrown schoolboy.

'How dare you scare me so!' I railed at him, pointing my finger. 'You frightened the life out of me.'

'Are you looking for the cave?' Alexander ignored my temper.

'Which cave?' In a contest between my temper and my curiosity, the latter wins every time. 'I did not know there was a cave on this hill.'

'Oh, yes.' Alexander's grin did not falter. 'It has quite a history. Have you ever read Blind Harry?'

I had to confess that I had not even heard of the gentleman.

'Blind Harry wrote about William Wallace, who was a patriot who fought the English...'

'I know who William Wallace was!' I had retained a fraction of my temper in case I needed to rebuke this man. I reminded him of the fact.

'Well,' Alexander was not one whit concerned about my temper. I knew then that I would require other methods to keep him under control. That was a strange thing to think about a man I had met only by chance. 'Blind Harry mentioned that Wallace sheltered in a cave on this hill.'

'Was he collecting plants by any chance?' I hoped to put this eager man in his place.

'No, indeed, he was fighting the English at the time.'

My words seemed to bounce off Alexander like hail off a stone wall. 'So where is this famous cave?' The thought came to me that my mysterious man may have been hiding in Wallace's Cave.

'Right here.' Alexander took hold of my cloak and nearly dragged me down the hill. Within a dozen steps, we were within one of the outcrops of rock I mentioned earlier. 'Can you see it?'

'No,' I wondered if Alexander was playing some prank on me.

'Here.' Letting go of my cloak, Alexander ducked behind a slanting grey rock and immediately vanished.

I followed. 'I passed right by this cave without seeing a thing.'

'William Wallace knew his stuff,' Alexander said. 'Blind Harry wrote that from here, Wallace fired arrows into Garleton Castle, just down there.'

I looked down into the ruined castle. 'I was there a few moments ago,' I said. 'I did not see this cave.'

'I was watching you,' Alexander said.

'You seem to spend a lot of time watching me,' I replied, crossly.

'You seem to be following me,' Alexander responded quickly. 'It is not intentional. You ran up Craigie Hill like a young deer.'

'Thank you.' *Was that a compliment?*

'I didn't know girls could move that fast.'

'Well, now you do.' I looked away. I was not sure how to react to Alexander Colligere. He was unlike any other man I had ever met.

I know that Craigie is not high, as hills are measured. It's like a pimple on a girl's bottom...'

'Alexander!' I stared at him, not sure whether to be shocked or to smile. 'You should not say such a thing in front of me!'

He looked at me and laughed. 'Why not? I'm sure you think the same.'

I looked away. 'I would never say that word.'

'Never? Not even to your most particular friend?'

I thought of Catherine Brown. Would I have said that word to her? I blushed at the memory of some of the conversations we had had when we were younger and discussed the men and marriages we hoped for. Yes, I would say that word and much worse to Catherine.

Alexander touched my shoulder. 'I did not mean to upset you.'

'I'm not upset,' I said. That was true. I was only surprised by my own false overreaction, not with Alexander's words.

We were quiet for a while as Alexander wondered if he had offended me and I wondered at the fragility of conventions that prevented us from speaking of things and feelings that we all share. I had never considered such a philosophy before.

'You are a strange man, Alexander.' I said at last.

'Most people think so,' Alexander agreed. 'I have learned to accept my eccentricities and hope that others do likewise.'

'Your Mr Ormiston seems to do so.'

'Wattie is a prince among men.' Alexander smiled. 'He talks as if he hates the world and acts as if he alone must save it and all inside it.'

I smiled at the description. 'Mr Ormiston has a wife and children.' Alexander nodded.

I was going to pursue that conversation until I realised Alexander had gone very quiet. He was looking anywhere except at me. Rather than him upsetting me, I had upset him. I did not know how or why.

'Show me around your cave, Mr Colligere.' I changed the subject onto something more comfortable for Alexander.

The cave was not extensive, merely a scrape in the rocks with an atmosphere that reeked of history. 'Do you like it?' Alexander sounded as proud as if he owned the place.

'I do,' I said.

We both heard the voices at the same time. 'Did you hear that?' I asked.

'The voices come from time to time,' Alexander said. 'If I had an imagination, I might think they were ghosts from the castle.'

'Or William Wallace come back to claim his own,' I smiled, thinking of the romantic novels I devoured when forced to stay indoors.

Alexander seemed very ready to smile. 'I had not thought of that.'

The voices sounded again, male and rough, with words that I certainly would not have liked my Mother to hear. Although, knowing her, she probably knew them all and had them catalogued, defined and ordered in a notebook in her immaculate copperplate writing.

'Did you see a man come out of this cave?' I asked.

Alexander shook his head. His clothes were a little ragged, I thought. His queue was unkempt, with loose hairs and the ribbon was untidy as if he had tied it in a hurry. He needed somebody to look after him, I thought vaguely. 'I've been in here since early morning,' he said, 'looking to see what manner of plants grow in the dark and cool.'

'I thought you said you were watching me.'

'Only by chance. I happened to look up, and there you were.'

The voices sounded again, a low grumble through the cave. 'Ghosts?' I hazarded. 'Fairies? People used to believe that fairies lived underground.' I screwed up my face until it became even uglier than it already was. 'I wonder if they can hear us as well.'

'We'll speak softly,' Alexander said.

'Maybe there is another chamber in this cave.' I said.

'I've checked,' Alexander shook his head. 'There is no second chamber.'

'I don't know then. I've run out of ideas.' I sat on a relatively flat rock. 'I know what it might be,' I said.

'What's that?' Alexander had found a tiny flower to examine.

'Witches.' I lowered my voice, trying to sound sinister. 'When I was a child I learned about the local witches. Well maybe the spirit of the East Lothian witches remains in this cave.'

I think that was the first time I saw Alexander lose his smile completely. 'I can't jest about witches,' he said. 'I knew one, once.'

About to attempt another joke, I saw sense in time. I wanted to ask Alexander about witches. I thought it best not to. 'I'm sorry, Alexander. I meant no offence.'

'Oh, it's all right.' Although Alexander attempted to bounce back immediately, his smile was crooked. 'You didn't offend me. You never offend me.'

'Not by intent, anyway,' I said. Alexander was like a puppy, I thought, all bright eyes and wagging tail, always wishing to be friendly.

'You can talk about witches if it pleases you,' Alexander said.

It did please me, of course. 'Only if you are sure.' I wanted to see why the subject vexed Alexander. 'If you don't wish to, then, why, we shall not.'

Alexander was silent for a long time. The only sound in that cave was our breathing.

'Who did you know that was a witch?' I asked the direct question.

Alexander's silence continued as I waited for an explanation. I think I would have waited until the cows came home with that stubborn man. I shook my head. 'It's all right, Alex. You don't have to tell me anything that makes you uncomfortable.'

'Yes, I can tell you.'

He was playing with words now. I wanted to know more. I wanted to know everything. Why? I was set on Captain Ferintosh was I not? My choice was between the bold captain or the balding old John Aitken. So why was I in the slightest interested in this eccentric plant collector? I liked him well enough, or at least I did not dislike him. But there was no more than that. After all, Alexander was hardly husband-material was he?

No: I was not interested in him as a man, I told myself. I was interested because of my natural curiosity. Nothing else.

'Would you tell me more?' I felt that I was torturing the poor fellow. Reaching forward, I touched his shoulder. 'No; forget I said that, Alexander. Let's talk about something else.'

Alexander breathed heavily. 'Yes I can tell you,' he said, ignoring my last statement. 'I don't like secrets.'

'Nor do I,' I said, thinking of the huge secret I was keeping from my parents. I felt sick with guilt at having freed Captain Ferintosh from the lock-up, just as I would have felt sick with guilt if I had the means to release him and I had left him there.

'I met a witch once,' Alexander said.

'There is more than that.' I felt that I knew this man. I could read his character well enough to know that he was hiding something from me.

'There is more than that.' Alexander sounded like the Spanish Inquisition was dragging the words from him by means of the rack and red-hot pincers. I realised that I was doing the dragging. I was acting the part of one of these sinister hooded figures from my childhood nightmares.

'Only tell me if you want to.' I pressed no further. I leaned back, allowing my question to penetrate Alexander's mind and work its way into his conscience.

About two minutes or a lifetime later, Alexander replied. 'I have not told many people.'

I nodded. 'I won't tell anybody else in the world.'

'I used to tell people.' The words came slowly. Alexander did not meet my gaze.

'Start at the beginning,' I advised. Something made me lean forward and touch Alexander's arm. 'Don't tell me if you don't want to.'

I already knew Alexander well enough to understand how he thought. If I pressed too hard; he would not say a thing. If I gave him time, he might relax sufficiently to tell me more.

'My mother was an herbalist,' Alexander said. 'It was she who taught me about plants.'

I nodded my encouragement.

'People used to seek her out for advice about things.'

'What sort of things?' While I sensed that Alexander wanted to talk but was afraid to do so, I guessed that he had spoken too much when he was younger, and others had responded with ridicule. 'It's all right, Alexander, you have no obligation to tell me anything.'

'How to find things that they lost and...' Alexander hesitated again.

'You can trust me,' I meant what I said.

'Some people, even married people, don't always get along well all the time.'

'Marriages have their good days and bad days.' I tried to hurry Alexander up. My impatience matches my temper.

Alexander lifted his chin again. 'My mother often gave advice to women who had problems in the bedroom.'

'I see.' I had no experience in such matters. Nor did I have any knowledge, except what I had gleaned from Catherine Brown. We had been two giggling youngsters, talking about subjects about which we knew little. Oh, we knew the mechanics of the thing, it was impossible to live in a farming community without understanding the basics of reproduction. The emotional side and the essence of love itself was as much a mystery as the man in the moon.

Alexander's smile was bright but forced. 'My mother's marriage was not of the best. I don't know the details.'

'No,' I said. 'Mothers don't often discuss their very personal business with their sons or daughters.'

'My mother warned me about marriages that don't work.' Alexander said. 'I told you that she was a healer. That is another word for a witch.'

I nodded. I knew all about the witches of East Lothian. It was an East Lothian witch coven that was reputed to have given King James VI the scare of his life, which may have contributed to the witch hunting epidemic that spread across all of King James's countries in the 17th century.

'Well, Mary, my mother did whatever witches do and wrote something on a piece of paper. I carry it with me all the time.' Reaching inside his sadly-battered cloak, Alexander produced a folded missive, heavily sealed with red wax, and tied with red ribbon.

'What's that?' I asked.

'It's the name of the only woman I can marry.' Alexander said.

I could not think what to say to that.

'My mother gave me this when she was on her deathbed.' Alexander lifted the packet. 'I am only to break the seal when I am certain I have found the right woman.' He shrugged. 'If the name inside here matches her name, we will be happy forever. If it does not match, we are destined for a miserable life.'

I still could not think what to say.

'Interesting eh?' Alexander tucked away his folded paper. 'As you can imagine, I am a bit wary of talking about witches.' His smile was lopsided. 'I am even more wary of becoming attached to a woman. Could you imagine how I would feel if I found a girl I thought was for me, opened the parchment and discovered the name did not match?'

'It could be your mother's way of ensuring that you choose carefully,' I said, thinking of Captain Ferintosh.

'It could,' Alexander said. 'Mother was not one to play games. She meant what she said.'

I thought again of my gallant captain. 'How often have you been tempted to open the paper and peek?'

Alexander shook his head. 'Never.' He said. 'I can only open it once.'

I thought about that for a few moments. 'I've never heard of anything like that before.'

'Neither have I,' Alexander said.

We were silent again. I could have asked more but, frankly, I did not consider Alexander's lack of a sweetheart to be any of my business. I had more than enough problems of my own.

As we sat there, we heard the voices once more.

'There they are again,' Alexander said.

'We might see more outside,' I suggested. 'Perhaps there is another cave or a secret passage from Huntlaw House.'

'Perhaps,' Alexander said. 'Although I've never heard of one.'

'Nor have I.'

A spatter of unseasonably early sleet greeted us as we left Wallace's Cave, forcing me to huddle deeper into my travelling cloak. 'Here,' Alexander passed over his comforter. 'Take this.'

'I don't need it.'

'You're cold,' Alexander pulled me into the shelter of a rock, opened my cloak and tied the comforter around my neck. I stood still and allowed him to care for me. Other men, even gentlemen, may have taken liberties. I knew Alexander would not. I hid my smile; I doubted Alexander had any inclinations towards women. Unless it had roots and green leaves, Alexander would have no interest at all. I was not surprised, after hearing about his queer mother.

'Thank you,' I said when I was tucked up to Alexander's satisfaction. 'That is very kind of you. Please don't get cold yourself, now.'

'I won't.' Alexander's smile was weak. 'I seldom feel the cold.'

About to ask why he wore a comforter then, I decided it was best to keep quiet. I waited until Alexander turned his back before I loosened the comforter sufficiently to allow me to breathe.

'Stand still!' Alexander's normally quiet voice cracked like the bark of a pistol. 'Listen!'

I could hear nothing except the spatter of sleet and whistle of wind on the rocks. 'What is it?'

'Something creaked.'

I listened for a creaking sound. 'Look!' I pointed. An entire section of the side of Craigie Hill lifted from the ground. 'What's that?'

'It's where the voices came from,' Alexander said at once.

It's where Captain Ferintosh disappeared to, I told myself. At the thought of that bold man, I felt my heart beat increase. I wondered if he was still there, under the ground only a few dozen yards from where I stood.

'Come on,' Alexander took hold of my arm. 'People who hide generally don't wish to be seen.' He guided me back to Wallace's Cave. 'It must be a trap-door to another cave. Maybe whisky smugglers use it.'

'Maybe they do.' I did not mention Captain Ferintosh. I hugged that secret to myself.

We crouched behind the rocks, scanning the hillside in case anything else untoward happened. Although I felt Alexander's body heat close by me, I thought of Captain Ferintosh and of John Aitken.

The ground opened again. Ready for it this time, I could see that there was a large wooden door so covered in turf that it merged with the surface of the hill. Inside the door, steps led downward. One man emerged, with grass spread over his green cloak. The second he appeared, the trap door closed again. I looked at the man in hope, but when I saw it was not Captain Ferintosh, I lost interest. Nearly invisible against the grey-green of the field, the man reached the road, brushed off the grass and walked away as if he had not a care in the world.

'Now that I have told you my story,' Alexander interrupted my observations. 'You can tell me yours.'

'My story?'

'Why you are wandering these hills all alone, watching that particular stretch of slope and studying every man who comes out.'

I sighed. The guilt was tearing at me. People say that a problem shared is a problem halved. I looked at Alexander with his laughing eyes; could I trust him? He had trusted me.

'I am looking for a man,' I said.

'Your sweetheart?' Alexander's question came quickly.

'I would like to think of him as such.'

'Ah.' Alexander smiled. 'You are not sure, then.'

Was I sure? 'No. I am not sure.'

Alexander looked away for a while. 'Am I correct in thinking your mysterious man may be hiding under the ground?'

'I think he may be.'

'There are only two reasons for doing that,' Alexander spoke slowly. 'Either he is hiding from authority, or he is authority, searching for a law-breaker.'

'Yes,' I said.

Alexander smiled. 'I think the secret I told you is safe with you, Mary. You don't give much away, do you?'

I took another deep breath. 'I don't know how much I can say,' I said. I was growing to like this man. I did not wish him to despise me for what I had done to my father.

'I won't force you to say anything,' Alexander lay back in our rocky lair. 'Let me tell you a story.'

'This is no time for stories,' I snapped, revealing the stretched state of my nerves.

'There is always time for a story,' Alexander said. 'You sit there, watch your wee bit ground in case your might-be-sweetheart appears and as you do so, listen to my golden voice.'

'You don't have a golden voice!'

'Silver, then.' Alexander was not in the least put off by my sharp response. If I had a brother, I would have treated him the same way, with familiarity and cutting words that were not intended to hurt. I looked at this strange man and hid my smile.

'Are you listening?'

'I don't appear to have much choice,' I said.

'You could leave the cave and walk away,' Alexander said.

I sighed. 'I'm listening.'

'Once there was a prince of thieves,' Alexander said. 'He was the most handsome of princes and the most charming of men. He roamed the countryside, doing illegal deeds and smiling his way out. Then one day he saw the most beautiful woman imaginable. Oh, but she was a peach, with her red hair and silky skin. He fell in love with her right away. What red-blooded man would not fall in love with her?'

I stirred slightly. 'I am a bit old for fairy stories.'

'You are never too old for fairy stories,' Alexander chided gently. 'No sooner had the prince given his heart to his lady love than the evil

94

sheriff captured him and threw him into the deepest darkest dungeon of his shire. The beautiful woman was distraught. What could she do?'

'What could she do?' I recognised the theme of Alexander's story. The pig was either guessing too much or knew me too well. 'I don't like this story very much.'

'Don't you? Then stand up and walk away,' Alexander said. 'I shall continue telling my tale to the bare stones in case the ghost of William Wallace is listening.'

'William Wallace has his own tales to tell.'

'He has indeed,' Alexander said. 'Shall I continue?'

'You will continue whether I wish you to or not.'

'That is true. What made the beautiful woman's dilemma even worse was that the evil sheriff was her father.'

'My father is not evil,' I said, hotly.

Alexander's smile broadened. 'So the beautiful woman had a terrible choice: she could go against her evil father by freeing the prince of thieves, or leave her sweetheart to rot in the darkest of dark dungeons. What a hard choice for a beautiful young woman.'

'I'm not beautiful.'

'Beauty is in the eye of the beholder,' Alexander said. 'Shall I leave the story there, or shall I continue.'

'Oh, continue, do.' I looked away. 'It's all stuff and nonsense, of course.'

'Of course, it is.' Alexander agreed. 'After agonising over her decision, the beautiful young woman with the auburn-red hair decided she must try to help her prince of thieves.'

'Did she indeed,' I put bitterness in my voice.

'Indeed she did,' Alexander's tone did not alter. 'Stealing a key...'

'Borrowing a key,' I amended. 'Stealing means to keep forever. Borrowing means to take and return.'

'Stealing a key, for stealing means to take without the owner's permission, the beautiful young woman freed the prince of thieves and helped him escape to a range of wild hills. She left him there, and the beautiful young woman was soon in trouble when a bunch of sorners arrived.'

'How do you know all this?' I demanded as my temper took control.

'Fortunately, a mysterious stranger saved her,' Alexander ignored my interruption. 'However, as soon as she returned to her cold-nosed castle, the beautiful young woman wondered if she had done the wrong thing. She wondered if her prince was as pure as she had thought. Yet she still wished to see him.'

I sat in silence, fuming as Alexander the pig unravelled me, strand by embarrassing strand.

'So she travelled to the place she had left him. There she met an ogre, a most ugly man with the face of a bear,'

'A pig more like. The face of a *pig!*' I emphasised my last word.

'A most ugly man with the face of a bear-pig who kept her trapped in his lair in the rocks.'

'That part is true, anyway,' I said.

'True? It is only a story!' Alexander smiled again.

'It is only a story,' I agreed. 'There is no auburn-haired beauty; there is no evil sheriff and no prince of thieves.'

'What there is,' Alexander's light tone deepened. He took hold of my arm, 'is a medley of voices.'

Chapter Ten

The voices were quite distinct, raised in animated discussion, perhaps even argument.

'Move to the back of the cave,' Alexander ordered, 'if you want to hear better.'

I scrambled over the rough rock with as little noise as possible. It was not far. I did not hear Alexander move, yet he was right beside me.

'Here,' he pointed to a deep cleft in the back of the cave. I eased in, gasping as the rock scraped against the tender skin of my thigh.

The voices were even more distinct now. There were three male voices and one female, with the occasional word drifting through like rocks in a swift Lammermuir stream. I listened.

'He's there!' I felt a surge of delight when I recognised Captain Ferintosh's tones. 'I can hear him speaking!'

Alexander did not reply. His gaze was fixed on my face. I could not read his thoughts.

I pressed my ear as close to the rock as I could. More words came through. One of the other men was talking. 'Highway.' 'Big House.' 'Coach.' 'Son.'

Individually the words meant nothing. I tried to make sense of them. Was Captain Ferintosh planning to drive his coach to a big house? Who was this son?

I placed my ear against the rock once more.

'Here,' Alexander was at my side, pressing against me as he worked at the edge of the rock with a knife. His lantern revealed a sight fissure, covered with earth. He scraped quietly to deepen the hole. I gasped as a pinprick of light shone through.

'Listen here,' Alexander whispered. 'But for goodness sake, don't make a noise.'

Unable to prevent myself, I pressed my eye to the tiny hole. At first, I could see nothing, and then gradually I worked out what was happening. The trapdoor must have led into quite a sizeable chamber under the hill, either natural or created by man at some time in the past. Two lanterns hung on hooks in the wall, pooling yellow light into an interior that looked surprisingly comfortable.

My limited view showed me two chairs and what might have been a shake-down bed, while the occasional person passed my line of sight.

There were four men, not three, and with a thrill of delight, I saw my Captain Ferintosh. He limped across in front of me, not as dapper as he once had been, but every bit as handsome and seemingly in control. The captain was speaking, moving his right hand in that characteristic way he had.

After a few moments of watching Captain Ferintosh, I adjusted my stance so I could hear what he was saying.

'Thursday morning.' Captain Ferintosh completed a sentence.

'Thursday morning,' one of the others said. I could almost taste the atmosphere within that queer little place.

I withdrew from the spyhole. That one sight of Captain Ferintosh had set my pulse racing. I did not know what it was about him that affected me in such a violent manner. It was not his poise: I had seen any number of the nobility on the streets of Edinburgh. They had equal dignity without disturbing my equanimity in the slightest. It was not the fact that he dressed immaculately: so did scores of other men to whom I would not give a second glance. No, I think it was the air of excitement, of daring, that clung to him.

I had to see him. Whatever happened, however much of a rogue he was, I had to see him. It is a measure of the trust I had for Alexander that I told him everything. I left out nothing. Alexander listened, nodding when I paused.

'It could be dangerous,' Alexander said at last. He neither criticised my judgement nor mentioned my misdemeanours.

'He won't hurt me,' I knew my captain. 'I will be perfectly safe with him.'

'What are you going to try to do?' Alexander looked concerned.

'I'm going to persuade him to come back into custody,' I told the whole truth. 'Father is the fairest man imaginable. He won't condemn anybody on the word of somebody else. I don't believe Captain Ferintosh is bad. I think he has got a bad reputation because of the company he keeps.'

Alexander raised his eyebrows. 'Would you like me to accompany you?'

I nearly fell off the rock on which I sat. 'No, thank you. I am quite capable of talking to Captain Ferintosh by myself.' The last thing I wanted was for another man to be present when I spoke to the captain.

'How will you contact him?' Alexander asked the next obvious question. 'You can hardly knock on the door and say: "Excuse me. I've been watching you in your secret hidey hole and want to meet you again."'

'No,' I said with a smile. 'There must be another way.'

'You said that Ferintosh met you in a coach,' Alexander said.

'A dark coach with gold trimmings,' I remembered. 'It was exquisite.'

'I'm sure it would be.' Alexander showed no jealousy over the captain's coach. 'We know that Ferintosh is living in a hole in the ground, so either his coach was hired, or somebody looks after it for him, or it is hidden away somewhere. He cannot ferret it away in his cave.'

I agreed although I was not sure where Alexander was leading me.

'Did it appear to be a hired coach?'

'No.' I said. 'It was beautiful. I've never known a stable to hire a coach of that quality.'

'From what you told me, I would agree.' Alexander said. 'That leaves us with two options. Either somebody is looking after his coach, or he has hidden it somewhere.'

'I think you are correct.' I was quite enjoying listening to Alexander's reasoning.

'Do we agree that Ferintosh is a rogue?' Alexander looked at me for confirmation.

'I think he must be,' I said with only a little reluctance.

'Then no respectable person would willingly hide his carriage. It will be close by so he can use it. You have great local knowledge, Mary. Do you know of anybody local who *would* allow Ferintosh to stable his coach and horses?'

'No.' I had no hesitation in replying. None of our neighbours would do such a thing.

'That leaves the last option,' Alexander said. 'He has his coach hidden somewhere.'

I had followed Alexander's reasoning with fascination. 'East Lothian is a big county; there are many places he can hide a coach.'

'It will be close by,' Alexander's constant smile was broadening as he spoke.

'Where close by? There is only Huntlaw House and Garleton Castle. I can't see Lady Emily agreeing to hide Captain Ferintosh's coach.' I smiled at the idea. 'That leaves the old castle.'

'Garleton Castle!' Alexander slapped his thigh resoundingly. 'Well now! It just happens that there is a coach in one of the ruined old buildings there.'

'What?' I stared at Alexander, unsure whether to be amused, irritated or just plain angry. 'You pig, Alexander Colligere! You knew all the time!'

'I did not,' Alexander denied hotly, grinning from ear to ear. 'I knew there was a carriage stowed away in Garleton Castle, but I did not know it belonged to Ferintosh.' He leaned back, evidently well pleased with himself. 'I would wager he stole it anyway, Mary.'

About to defend Captain Ferintosh in the strongest possible terms, I saw the sudden seriousness in Alexander's face and snapped shut my mouth. Perhaps my roguish captain *had* stolen the coach.

'Are you sure you wish to meet this fellow?' Alexander asked. 'He does not seem to sail with the right wind. I mean, he could lead you into serious trouble.'

I knew that. I knew that I was putting myself into grave danger. Perhaps it was the thrill of excitement that encouraged me, or the comparison between the rogue and the staid, balding John Aitken.

'I'm sure I want to meet him.'

'Well then, why not leave a note on his carriage? The last time he decided where to meet you. This time you choose. Make him come to you.'

I nodded. 'I rather like the idea.' I would choose a place I knew well. 'Alexander; why are you helping me?'

Alexander looked away. 'We are friends I hope.'

'I hope so too,' I said.

I felt the strangest sensation as I said that. Here I was, telling a virtual stranger about my planned assignation with a fugitive. Yet, I knew I could trust Alexander with my secret. Perhaps because he had been honest with me, I felt I could tell him anything.

'Thank you, Alexander.'

I swear that he blushed. 'There's nothing to thank me for. That's what friends do, I think.'

'It is,' I said. That last phrase, *I think*, had told me more about this man. I had a sudden vision of his life, a man who thought different from his peers, a man who would undoubtedly be tormented at school because of his eccentricities. From what I knew of people, they banded together and delighted to torment anybody that dared to be different.

'You are more than a friend, Alexander. You are a *true* friend.' I said.

'You'll need a pen and paper.' Alexander ignored my last words. 'Here.' Reaching inside his cloak, he produced a small rosewood box, which, when opened, proved to be a writing set complete with pen, ink, blotter and a pad of paper.

'What else do you have, you amazing man?' I had never met a man who carried such a thing as a writing set with him.

'It's for my notes,' Alexander seemed almost guilty as he explained. 'When I find interesting plants I write their description, where I found them, that sort of thing.'

'You are the most wonderful man,' I said. Leaning forward, I kissed him, lightly, on the forehead. It was the sort of kiss one gives to one's father or brother, if one has such an entity. In this case, it made Alexander recoil in what seemed like horror.

'Alexander?' I paused in genuine concern.

Astonishment had replaced his smile. He touched his forehead. 'Thank you.'

'It was only a kiss,' I said, 'between friends. Come on, Alexander. If you please, could you help me write my missive?'

Alexander's usual eloquence had deserted him along with his smile. 'I don't know.' He touched his forehead again. 'You might write: "I must meet you on a matter of the greatest urgency?"'

'Thank you, Alexander,' I said. 'Now, unless you lose your Friday face, I will kiss you again.'

My words brought his smile back. 'You are a little minx when you choose to be.'

'We're a fine pair, then,' I said. 'You are a pig while I am a minx.'

'A fine pair indeed,' Alexander shook his head. 'Now, you add where and when you wish to meet your sweetheart.'

'I'm not sure he is my sweetheart, my betrothed or only a friend,' I said, absent-mindedly chewing the end of Alexander's pen. I removed a barb from between my teeth.

I could not read the expressions that crossed Alexander's face. 'I thought it was all confirmed, Mary. Why is there the confusion?'

Without repeating the name Edmund, I explained about Captain Ferintosh's statements about trusting me with his name.

'That could mean anything,' Alexander spoke slowly, as if he were thinking about every word. 'Or it might mean nothing.'

I nodded. 'We agree on that, too.'

Alexander looked thoughtful. 'Come on, Mary, finish off your note. We'll attach it to Ferintosh's chariot and then get you back home.'

Without much thought, I added "meet at the lone pine tree on the fringe of Lammermuir at 10 tomorrow night." The tree was quite distinctive; all I had to do was slip out of the house unobserved again. It was fortunate that Cauldneb was old, with crooked rooms, including my bedroom, in unusual situations.

'Come on, Mary,' Alexander interrupted my train of thought. 'I'll show you where the chariot is.'

If Alexander had not told me, I would never have discovered the carriage. Garleton Castle was a ruin, but some of the chambers – I hesitate to call them rooms – remained surprisingly watertight.

'What on earth were you doing, poking about in here?' I looked around the dark chamber into which Alexander had brought me.

'Searching for lichens,' Alexander had a lantern, which he shone on the bodywork of the coach. 'Was that your chariot, Mary?'

I must confess to having no interest in carriages. I know some are more luxurious than others, some have different shapes, some are open, and others closed. I opened the door. 'Yes, this is Captain Ferintosh's coach.' I remembered the luxurious scent of soft leather.

'Or the carriage that Ferintosh used.' Alexander's voice was so low I could hardly hear it.

'Yes.' I said.

'Ferintosh might not be using the carriage for days or weeks,' Alexander said. 'But even he will have to feed the horses. They are down that way.' He nodded to an adjacent chamber.

'I'll leave the note beside the horses,' I said, stepping back. 'Thank you, Alexander.'

He caressed his forehead again. 'Once we've left the note, I'll have to take you home, Mary.'

I nodded, wondering what this complex man was thinking. About to say that I knew the way, I bit off the words. I had no objection to Alexander's company. He distracted me from my more pressing worries about Captain Ferintosh and Mr John Aitken.

At the entrance to the castle, a dog rose bush clung to the ancient stones. Ragged with age and tormented by the wind, it still possessed a form of beauty. I caressed it as I passed, enjoying the example of nature's ability to survive in even the most unlikely of locations. Low down, a single pink rose braved the lateness of the season. I plucked the rose, sniffed the residual scent and passed it over to Alexander.

'I cannot thank you for your help,' I said. 'So here is a rose to remember me by.'

Alexander took the rose as if it were the most precious gift in the world. 'There is no need,' he said. 'I will never forget you.'

I smiled, turned away and immediately forgot the incident. It had been a passing fancy, a gesture that meant nothing to me.

Alexander touched my arm. 'Come on now, Mary. It's time you were safe in bed.'

The second that Alexander left me at the gates of Cauldneb, my spirits plummeted at the thought of John Aitken. When I turned to wave goodbye, Alexander was still there, watching me every step of the way home.

Chapter Eleven

Ignoring my nagging conscience, I was becoming quite adept at sneaking out of the house at night. Wearing my usual dark clothing, with Father's tricorne hat on my head, I travelled my usual route out the side door into the biting darkness of the night. Having learned from past experience, I carried a lantern to enable me to see the path and a stout stick for protection.

I knew the path well from our house to the edge of the policies. Beyond that, I was not quite so certain. I had deliberately chosen a site on the fringes of Lammermuir, but I hurried there with an occasional stumble over hidden rocks and tangled heather. All the time I wondered if my captain would turn up. I trusted him, of course, but he was a fugitive from justice. Would he venture so close to the house of a magistrate? I hoped so. I hoped his love for me would encourage him to brave my father's dark house.

The lone pine thrust starkly on the southern slope of the muir. Winter-bare, its branches reached upward in supplication to the cloud-heavy sky. Pulling my hat down and wrapping Alexander's comforter closer around my neck, I panted up the heather slope until I was within ten yards of the tree.

'Captain Ferintosh,' I whispered the name, then louder: 'Captain Ferintosh!'

Nothing answered except the wind, rustling the branches like the whisper of a condemned man. Now shivering, I lifted my lantern, allowing the light to probe into the dark.

'It would be better if that light was doused, Miss Hepburn!' Captain Ferintosh appeared from behind the tree. He was back to his dapper self, with a silver-mounted tricorne hat above a long, dark blue cloak. 'A light can be seen for miles at night.'

'Yes, Captain.' I hurriedly pulled the shutter, hiding the light.

I heard, rather than saw, Captain Ferintosh come closer.

'Captain,' I waited for him to embrace me. He did not.

'What is it, Miss Hepburn? Why do you wish urgently to see me?' The captain's voice was clipped, quite unlike his usual well-modulated tones.

'I wish to see you all the time,' I said, truthfully.

'Is there a reason for this meeting?' The captain was agitated, perhaps not surprisingly given his situation.

'It is mostly because I wanted to see you again,' I said.

Captain Ferintosh shook his head. 'Do you realise that I am a wanted fugitive? Half the county is hunting for me. I am a man outside the law.'

'I don't care,' I said. 'I still want to see you.' I took a deep breath as I threw my caution to the cold Lammermuir wind. 'Don't you realise, Captain Ferintosh, Edmund Charleton or whatever your real name is, that I still love you?'

There: the words were out in the open. I had laid my ace of hearts on the table and waited to see if the captain held the same suit in his hand. I lifted my chin to await his response.

'Yes, yes,' Captain Ferintosh brushed aside my declaration as if it was of no importance to him. 'But what was the matter of the greatest urgency that compelled you to arrange this meeting?'

'Pray sir,' I felt my famous temper rising. 'Did you not hear me? I said that I loved you.'

'Yes, I heard you,' Captain Ferintosh controlled his nerves. 'I am much obliged, Miss Hepburn.' I saw the flash of his teeth, white through the night.

'I ask a kiss, sir, before we continue.' I tried to press my case. I was well aware that he might not find my next suggestion favourable so I desired to put him in the best possible humour before I approached that most uncomfortable subject.

'A kiss?' Captain Ferintosh's voice rose in disbelief. That was not at all the reaction I hoped for. 'Madam: Miss Hepburn.'

'You used to call me Lady Mary,' I reminded. 'I have no objections to you returning to that mode of address.'

Captain Ferintosh took an audible deep breath. 'My sweet Lady Mary, I am a hunted man. The longer I remain in any one place, the more danger I am in.'

'Then kiss me quickly, sir, and hear what I have to say,' I was not inclined to back down.

'Oh, good God!' Bending forward, Captain Ferintosh pecked me on the lips. 'There now, say what you have come to say.'

I bit back my disappointment. 'It is this, sir. You are aware that my father is a magistrate.'

'I am aware of that,' Captain Ferintosh started as a vixen barked somewhere in the low country.

'It's only a fox,' I said, somewhat impatiently, 'not a company of dragoons!'

'Speak, madam!'

'Well, Captain Ferintosh. My father is the fairest of men. If you give yourself up voluntarily, I will also speak a good word for you. I know Father will give you a fair trial without prejudice. You will be found not guilty and can be free to walk abroad in daylight.'

I could not see the expression on Captain Ferintosh's face although I was sure he was considering my proposition in all seriousness. I waited, expecting his gratitude and assent.

'Indeed, Captain,' I pursued what I hoped was my advantage. 'I can take you to my father now, right this minute, and if you give your parole, as I am sure you shall, you can spend the night in our house of Cauldneb rather than in chains in Muirend lockup.'

I could not say fairer than that.

For some reason, Captain Ferintosh did not agree. 'You brought me up here for that tomfool idea?' I had never heard him angry since the first day we met. Now his temper was directed at me. 'You are asking me to place my neck in your father's noose?' For a horrible moment, I thought he would strike me.

'Father will not hang an innocent man,' I said, now trembling. I wished I had not come. I wished I had not tried to help. I wished I had minded my own business. 'Please, Captain Ferintosh.'

I sensed him controlling his temper. I heard him draw in his breath. 'Miss Hepburn,' he spoke with something of his old tones. 'You are a brave young woman to come to me with this suggestion in the middle of the night.'

That was better. My captain's nerves must have been stretched beyond endurance for him to act as he had been.

'I hope you can forgive my loss of temper, Lady Mary.'

'There is nothing to forgive, sir,' I said at once. 'There is no need for apologies between people in love.' I hesitated for only a minute. 'You do love me, don't you?'

'Lady Mary,' Captain Ferintosh stepped closer. I inhaled the rich scent of tobacco from his cloak. 'If I did not love you, I would not have come here tonight.'

I allowed his words to wrap around me. His arms were next, strong and secure. I closed my eyes as he kissed me.

'I thank you for the suggestion, Lady Mary,' Captain Ferintosh murmured in my ear, 'but I cannot do as you wish.' The sensation of his kiss lingered on my lips.

When he released me, I stood still for quite some time. 'Captain Ferintosh?' I spoke only to the tree. There was nobody else on that hill slope except me.

'No! Don't leave me alone again!'

You may think me naïve to fall for such a man. I was naïve, but many women have done the same. Surrounded by mediocre uniformity, when something or someone different comes into our life, we can look for adventure in the belief that they share the love that we feel, or that we think we feel. At twenty, I had been exposed to only a limited circle of people, my father's friends and their immediate family. They were mostly from farming stock, with a few minor military officers who remained for a few months before being posted abroad. Captain Ferintosh was unlike anybody I had ever met before.

At twenty I knew that I was approaching the age of consent and marriage. Within a few months, at the very most a couple of years, my parents would have me engaged to what they perceived as a suitable husband. After marriage, I would be stifled in respectable conformity for the remainder of my life. When my mother suggested Mr John Aitken as suitable husband material, can you wonder that I leapt at the most opposite personality possible?

I was wrong. Even then, as I pursued Captain Ferintosh, I knew that I was being foolish. I could not have imagined what life would be like attached to such a man. A man who lived on the hazy border between law and outlaw, who walked with a swagger, smiled readily, had the respect of all who knew him and spent money more lavishly than any penny-pinching farmer I had ever known.

Looking back now, with a smile on my face, perhaps I can understand why I lifted my skirt above my ankles and followed Captain Ferintosh down that steep Lammermuir slope, with my lantern bouncing from my left hand and my staff thump-thump-thumping on the heather.

I saw Captain Ferintosh's form as he rose to the crest of a slight ridge, sharp against a hazy moon. I did not shout; I remembered his warning about light travelling far at night and realised that sound would be equally revealing. The captain was moving quickly, his long legs striding over the heather and onto the grass of the outfields where Father's cattle would habitually have grazed.

With my long skirt hindering me, I lifted it high above my knees to move the faster. With nobody to see me, there was no need to worry about either dignity or respectability. Revelling in my new freedom, I nearly ran, cutting the distance to the captain.

I was right about sound carrying in the night. A few moments after the captain disappeared over the ridge, I heard the voices. I slowed down at once, thinking that somebody had caught Captain Ferintosh. I hefted my staff, ready to leap to his rescue, until the female laugh cut through the dark, and through my heart.

'She's a silly little thing,' Captain Ferintosh said. 'Harmless, but silly.'

'What did she have to say for herself?' That was the female voice, sharp-toned.

'She said I should hand myself into her Father for a fair trial.'

I stiffened in disbelief. *These people were talking about me. Captain Ferintosh thought I was silly. Who was this woman?* I tried to peer into the dark.

'Did she tell you anything we can use?'

'Nothing at all.' Captain Ferintosh said. 'It was a wasted trip.'

I told you that I loved you, I said to myself. *Did that mean nothing?* Perhaps he did not wish the woman to know that. I deluded myself again. I followed them at a distance, walking slowly, feeling miserable, and wishing I was in my warm bed.

I heard the clatter of metal on metal. 'Halloa, Captain.' That was a man's voice, uneducated, guttural.

'Jack.' One sharp word from Captain Ferintosh.

With clouds now covering the moon, there was no light. I tried to peer into the dark. I could not see anything.

Something hard pressed into my back and a rough hand closed over my mouth. 'And what are you snooping after, my lad!'

That was the third time I had been grabbed by somebody in the last week, but the first time anybody had ever mistaken me for a man. It must have been the tricorne hat or perhaps the cloak that concealed my shape; either way, I was most put out. I have nothing of the man about me. I have all the attributes that a woman should have, perhaps more plentiful that I would like in certain places.

The man dragged me away. 'If you make one sound I'll blow your backbone into the next field.'

As I had no intention of being parted from my backbone, I took my captor's advice and remained mute. With his great paw across my mouth, I had no other option.

It is strange that in novels, highwaymen are romantic heroes, prostitutes have hearts of gold and rogues in the countryside are rough-hewn on the outside and decent fellows underneath. Unfortunately for romantic novels, the reality is nothing like that. In my limited experience with the breed, highwaymen are violent thieves with a horse, prostitutes are bedraggled and broken women, and rogues in the countryside are as heartless as any from the foulest dens in the city.

'Here, Captain;' my captor thrust me in front of him. 'I found this lad following you.' My captor proved to be a thick-set man in middle years with a large pistol.

Captain Ferintosh took one look at me and swore. Why men have to swear so often, I do not know. I am glad that women have not adopted that most demeaning habit. 'That's not a boy, that's a blasted woman.'

'It's me,' I said helpfully.

'Is this Andrew Hepburn's girl?' The woman stepped closer to me. 'Is this the one who wanted to see you?'

'That's her.' Captain Ferintosh said.

'Bring her along.' The woman said. 'We'll decide what to do with her later.'

Now in all the best romances, either I would have made a dash for freedom, or gallant Captain Ferintosh would have spoken up in my defence. In reality, with an ugly brute of a man holding a pistol a few inches from my back, I was too scared to do anything except comply. As for Captain Ferintosh, well, he did as he was told as well. He certainly said nothing to help me.

'Where are we going?' I asked.

I found out soon enough as we returned to that trapdoor in the hill. The man they called Jack shoved me through the entrance. I fell onto the hard ground, to find two other men staring at me.

'Who's he?'

'It's a woman,'

'Then why is she wearing a man's hat.' One of the men flicked off my father's hat. 'She's a redhead.' He said, unnecessarily as my hair flopped over my face.

'She was following us,' the woman said. 'Tie her up.'

I was going to protest until Jack stuck the muzzle of his pistol against my throat. I decided it was better to co-operate. Tied wrist and ankle, I was pushed to the ground with a painful thump. I sat against the rock-hewn side of that strange place with my heart pounding as if it would escape from my chest. I was scared. I was more scared than I had ever been in my life. I did not understand what was happening and still hoped that Captain Ferintosh would help me.

They stood over me, Jack, two men I did not know, Captain Ferintosh and the woman. I tried to smile to the woman, hoping for some comfort from a member of my own sex. I would have been as well to whistle for the man in the moon. I have never seen such established cruelty as there was in her face. I would guess she was in her late twenties but every year must have been hard and bitter to judge by the engraved lines around her mouth. Her eyes, narrow and vicious, bored into me with the force of a gimlet.

'What will we do with this?' She kicked me, directing the question to Captain Ferintosh.

The captain looked at me dispassionately. 'Keep her for now. She might be useful.'

'For what?' The woman snapped.

'A lever.' I did not recognise the captain's smile. 'If any of us are arrested, having a magistrate's daughter as a hostage might help. What respectable man would sentence a prisoner knowing his kith and kin would suffer?'

The woman kicked me again. She seemed to enjoy that. 'It would not affect you, Edmund. You would sell your mother for half a guinea.'

'I would sell her for half a crown,' the captain said. 'But I'm not respectable.'

I had never been in the company of such people before. Frankly, I was petrified. I know that in romantic novels, women might scream for help or break their bonds or somehow wriggle free. Well, let me tell you that there is nothing romantic about such people, screaming would not help, and Jack was an expert bond-fastener. My wrists were as well secured as a ship on a stormy night.

The woman bent closer, fixing me with a glare. 'If you give me any trouble, you...' She called me a name I had never heard used before. 'I will make sure you long for death.' Lifting her skirt to expose her thighs in a most shocking manner, she produced a long-bladed knife. 'I'll scar that pretty face of yours so that even your own mother will shudder to look at you.'

I believed her. Anybody with eyes like hers was capable of any depravity. It was not stubborn pride that prevented me from replying, but pure fear. She kicked my hip, hard.

'Leave her, Isabel,' Captain Ferintosh said. 'We have more important things to do than torment a child.'

Isabel? I would remember that name. Scared as I was, I had not given up hope. I intended to survive this ordeal. For the first time, I believe that I understood how important my father's position as a magistrate was. Oh, I know that most of his cases consisted of petty poaching, minor affray and the like, but he also protected the good people of East Lothian from the genuine rogues such as these. And most people are good; I still believe that. Few are perfect, we all have our quirks, but there is genuine kindness in most people.

I could not see any of that kindness in Isabel.

What had the captain called me? A child? For some reason that seemingly innocent word, child, destroyed my last fragment of affection for the man. He did not view me as a woman even. He had been using me.

I closed my eyes. Was there some way out of this?

I worked out that this cave must have been part of Wallace's Cave once. At some time in the past, there had been a rock fall that divided the cave into two chambers, leaving this, much larger one, isolated within the hillside. The captain and his gang, or perhaps an earlier outlaw band, had created the secret opening and now it formed an almost perfect hideaway.

Despite the murmur of conversation continuing, punctuated by vile language and raucous laughter, I was nearly sleeping as mental and emotional exhaustion overcame me.

'Speak quietly; she'll hear.'

I heard the words through the miasma of sleep.

'It's sleeping.' Every one of Isabel's words seemed as cutting as the blade of her knife.

'Get some rest. Tomorrow will be a busy day.' Captain Ferintosh said. 'If you remember your parts we'll be fine. The old woman is as dottery as a rotten cabbage. Isabel and I will do the talking. You three are our servants.'

'Why do I have to be a servant?'

I heard a sharp slap and jerked my head up. Jack was holding his face as Isabel pressed her face against his. 'You'll do as you're damned well told,' she hissed. 'You haven't the wit to pull this off.'

Jack lowered his hand, nodding. The others watched, the captain with a whimsical smile playing at the corners of his mouth. I closed my eyes again, listening.

What did they intend? Who was the dottery old woman?

'We'll arrive before dawn,' Captain Ferintosh said. 'They won't be properly awake then so we'll catch them unawares.'

'Do we have to call you My Lord?' Jack seemed to have recovered from Isabel's slap.

'Yes.' Captain Ferintosh said. 'If you call me Captain, by God you'll regret it for the rest of your life.'

'If any of you fail us,' Isabel's voice was like the kiss of the devil, 'I'll personally take care of you.'

I shivered at the menace of her words.

'What about that?' I knew Isabel was referring to me.

'Leave her here.' Captain Ferintosh said.

'I say we cut its throat.' Isabel said casually. 'I doubt it will be any good to us.'

'It's insurance,' the captain said. 'You know that I like to have an escape plan.'

Isabel approached me once more. 'Did you hear that?' I expected her vicious kick.

I nodded.

'Good. The captain wants to keep you alive. I don't care one way or the other.' She leaned close to my face again. 'I would slit your throat and sleep easy.'

I mustered up as much courage as I could, forcing myself to meet her poisonous glare. 'Murdering a helpless woman is about your level,' I tried to keep the tremor from my voice. 'You'll never achieve anything higher.'

Her slap knocked me sideways; I winced at the kicks on my legs, hips and side.

'We could take her with us,' Jack said.

'We leave it behind,' Isabel landed one last, savage, kick. 'You've got altogether too much to say for yourself, Jack Samson.'

Jack Samson. I stored that name in my mind. When I got away, if I got away, I would make sure that Father had the names of Isabel and Jack Samson. The thought of Father brought a host of new thoughts crowding into my head. Soon they would discover that I was gone. They would be worried sick about me.

It was easier to remain lying than to struggle to a sitting position. I watched as Captain Ferintosh changed into the finery I remembered so well. I had never seen a man dress before, with Isabel helping him strip to his underwear and then put on layer after layer. He wore a silk shirt with many ruffles at the sleeves, skin-tight breeches that left little to the imagination, a bright blue-and-silver waistcoat, and then a silk cravat. Isabel tied that too, taking care over the procedure. She made an excellent job of it too, I admitted grudgingly. Finally, the captain donned a royal blue overcoat with golden buttons.

'I wish we had real gold,' Isabel fingered one of the buttons.

'Pinchbeck will have to do,' Captain Ferintosh said. 'The old crow won't know the difference, or she won't care.'

Which old crow? In this agricultural area, the only elderly woman who may be interested in the difference between real gold and pinchbeck was Lady Emily. Why on earth would Captain Ferintosh wish to go to Huntlaw? Was he planning to rob the house? If so, why the fancy clothing?

With golden buckles on his shoes, gold braid on his tricorne hat and a gold-topped cane, Captain Ferintosh looked every inch the dandy. Beau Brummell would not have looked at him, of course, but for our rural corner of the world, he was a sparkling diamond among the earthy farmers.

As the captain was dressing, the other men had been busy changing as well. For a few moments, I had the less-than-pleasant experience of being in close company with three near-naked men. It was the sort of scene that Catherine Brown and I had giggled over as young teenagers. The reality was not so agreeable, or so easy on the eye. The men emerged as footmen, dressed in brown uniforms that did not alter the ugliness of their appearance one whit.

Finally, Isabel dressed. Completely unabashed by the male company, she stripped to her petticoats and pulled on a gown of dark green, set with ruffles. It was plainer than I had expected, while the cumbersome string of pearls she draped around her neck was more suited for a farmer's wife than the companion of a man as splendid as the captain appeared. I frowned; the pearls probably had belonged to a farmer's wife a few days ago.

What on earth was the Captain planning?

Pulling on a green travelling cloak with a lined hood, Isabel nodded to the rest. 'Time we were away.' She gave me a parting kick. 'Check this thing's bonds are secure, Jack, and follow us.'

Jack knelt over me, tugging at the ropes that chafed my wrists and ankles. 'You'll keep,' he said, allowing his hands more leeway than I cared for as they ran up my legs. 'Don't go running off now, my pretty one. I have a better use for you than the captain has planned.'

'That'll be my Lord Captain,' I tried to kick at him for, in truth; he was only a brainless brute. He did not scare me half as much as Isabel did. My kick failed. It may be possible in romantic theory, but when one is tied, movement is not easy.

'We'll be back, my fancy,' Jack's breath was foul as he leaned over me. 'Don't go thinking of escape now. The door is bolted from the outside.' He lowered his voice. 'You're all alone, little red-haired princess.' He patted my backside, squeezed my breast painfully and left me alone with my thoughts.

Now, you may think that being tied up is nothing to worry about. Let me tell you that it is terrible torture in itself. The ropes chafe at wrists and ankles, the tightness constricts the flow of blood so the hands and feet swell and the inability to move leads to terrible cramps. I had been lying on my side for what seemed like hours, with the pressure on my right hip giving me increasing pain.

I struggled to a sitting position. The dark pressed down on me. There is no dark quite like the darkness within one's head when trapped in an unlit underground chamber in a Scottish November. Without even a peep of light and with chilling cold seeping into that part of me then pressing against the chill of the ground, I literally sobbed with discomfort and mental anguish.

'Get hold of yourself,' I said severely. 'Worse things happen at sea. What would Mother do?' The answer was simple. Mother would not be so stupid as to get herself into such a situation in the first place. 'Well,' I said. 'That was no help at all.' I wriggled to try and restore some feeling into my now-numb nether regions. It was not very ladylike perhaps, but necessary in such a situation.

Using the wall as a lever, I forced myself upright to relieve the pressure. I was nearly standing when I overbalanced and fell face forward; sprawling over the table I had forgotten was there.

'Now there's a picture I will never forget!' The voice boomed from nowhere. With my face down and other parts elevated, I was momentarily unable to move. A light shone around me as that same voice sounded again. 'Don't you worry Miss Hepburn; I'll have you out of there in a few moments.'

Chapter Twelve

'Who are you?' I asked, thinking the unknown man could hardly have caught me in a more undignified position.

'A friend. We've met before.'

I heard a terrible rumbling sound, I choked in a sudden cloud of dust, and then a pair of hands restored me to an upright position. The glow of a lantern gave welcome light, and I saw the blackened forehead and eyes of the man who had rescued me on a previous occasion. From the nose down, a kerchief covered his face as though he were Dick Turpin.

'Who are you?'

'A friend.' The man repeated. He sawed at my bonds with a knife.

I gasped as the ropes parted. The return of circulation was agonising. I writhed as the man knelt at my feet. 'Pray permit me.' He rubbed at my ankles, easing the pain, and performed the same operation to my wrists and hands.

'Thank you,' I looked around. My rescuer had burrowed in from Wallace's Cave, shoving aside one of the rocks that had fallen in the distant past. That had been the rumbling sound.

My rescuer spoke again. 'We'd better get clear of here. These rocks are creaking. They might collapse again at any time.'

I did not resist as he took hold of my wrist and guided me out of that hellish chamber, into Wallace's Cave and out into the open air. I took a deep breath of the pre-dawn crispness.

'Who are you?' I asked for the third time. With his face concealed and the kerchief muffling his voice, I did not recognise one little bit about him. 'I thought I knew all the local men; you are not one of them.'

'Come on. We'll get you home before your mother discovers you are adventuring again.' His hand was firm on my wrist.

'No.' I had made a decision in my time in the cave. 'I have had enough of deception and acting. I want things out in the open.'

My companion stopped. 'That will lead you into a great deal of trouble.'

I knew that. 'It will clear my conscience,' I said.

'That may be very commendable. It will also hurt your mother and father to know that you have been deceiving them, that you released Captain Ferintosh from prison and that you met him secretly. Do you want to hurt your parents?'

'No.' I had put myself in another dilemma.

'I did not think so. Better to let sleeping dogs lie.' My companion said.

'How much do you know?' I asked.

'Between the pair of us, we probably know quite a bit.'

'Captain Ferintosh is planning a robbery I think,' I blurted out. 'He is dressed like a gentleman and is going to the house of an old lady.'

'Do you know who?'

'Not for sure. I think it might be Lady Emily.' I hesitated a little. 'He was less than complimentary about an old lady, but I think he meant her Ladyship.'

My companion grunted. 'All right. I will call round to Cauldneb tomorrow to speak to your father, Miss Hepburn.'

I felt an immediate flutter of alarm. 'Who are you, sir?'

'You'll find out tomorrow. In the meantime, we'll get you back home.'

'That's twice you've rescued me,' I said. 'You are my white knight, my Sir Lancelot of the Lake.'

'I am neither of these things.' My knight's voice was curt and very Scottish. He did not sound like I imagined Sir Lancelot to be. 'Get home and get some sleep.'

Chapter Thirteen

As you may imagine, I was tired the next morning, or rather, later that same morning. I also had to hide the raw marks on my wrists and ankles where the bonds had chafed the skin. When I am tired, I also get grumpy, or *crabbit,* as we say in this part of the world, so I gruffed at Maggie, snapped at the footman and was surly with my mother, which is never the best idea.

'You look peaky,' Mother said. 'I'll get a tonic for you.'

Mother had the most basic ideas about health. She could also be obsessed with the movement of bowels, speaking of them in the most forward manner, whatever the company. Either that or she was deliberately humiliating me as punishment because I was out of temper. In my day, a tonic was the universal cure for many things, as seawater was the panacea for seamen.

'Mother!' I snapped back at her. 'Don't say such things.'

'Oh, stuff and nonsense, Mary Agnes!' Mother's look was a mixture of irritation and amusement. 'We all have bowels. There is no need to hide such things from Maggie Is there, Maggie?'

Maggie bobbed in a curtsey. She was about thirteen years old and had a whole brood of siblings, who doubtless also had bowels. 'Indeed not Mrs Hepburn. My ma says that if we look after our insides, the outsides will also be healthier. Shall I fetch the tonic, Mrs Hepburn?' I could sense the triumph in the look Maggie threw at me. After I grumphed at her, she probably wished to administer the dose herself, making it extra large so I spent the entire morning perched uncomfortably on the chamber pot.

'No, thank you, Maggie. Mary is quite capable of looking after her health.'

'Thank you, Mother.' In truth, I felt anything but healthy. My head was thick with tiredness, half my muscles were aching with the exertions of the previous night while my wrists and ankles were burning. Worst of all was my worry about this man who had promised or threatened to visit that morning. Who was he and what trouble would his revelations uncover? I wished, I desperately wished, that I had never ventured into this murky business with Captain Ferintosh and his merry men.

'There now Mary, take a dish of tea with your kippers,' Now that her point had been proved, Mother was quite prepared to be magnanimous. I will give her that, she never held a grudge or rubbed in her victories. She never had to, I suppose because there were so many of them. Only father ever defeated her in an argument, and then only rarely.

'I am glad to hear that you and John Aitken get along so famously.' Once again Mother proved her skill in catching me off guard. I had nearly forgotten about balding-John in all the other excitements. Have you ever noticed that about life? It jogs along with nothing much happening for months, and then, suddenly, everything happens at once. Only a few weeks back I had nothing bothering my mind, except mundane household matters, and now there was a proposed marriage to a bald old man, Captain Ferintosh and his terrifying woman Isabel, this mysterious fellow with the blackened face and even Alexander Colligere. There was too much happening.

'Well?' Mother was staring at me. I had drifted away into a *dwam*, as we term a daydream.

'Yes,' I said.

'Yes? Is that all you have to say for yourself?'

'Yes, we got on all right.' I was not sure what I was expected to say.

'I heard that you got on better than that.'

'Oh.' I presumed that John Aitken had reported back to Mother. Strangely, I had expected better of him than that. He did not strike me as the sort of man who would go running with tales. Still, we live and learn. I added that little tit-bit to my store of information. It was one more reason why I had no desire to marry that sometimes-pleasant old man.

We all heard the bells ringing at the same time. I looked at Mother, all disagreements forgotten.

'Good Lord in heaven!' Maggie said. 'Whatever is that?'

'It's a bell,' I said. 'Somebody is ringing a church bell.'

'But it's Thursday.' Rising from the table, Mother stepped to the window. 'There's no service on a Thursday and certainly no wedding at this time in the morning.' I thought she might take the opportunity to comment about my intended marriage, but she spared me that torture. 'It's not the king's birthday is it?'

Father burst into the room, looking as equally out of temper as I was. He was bare-necked, with his shirt incorrectly buttoned. 'What the devil is all that noise? Can't a man get any peace in his own house? Good God! Have the French landed? We're not in another blasted war, are we? It's only a few years since the last one! They might at least let a fellow know!'

'No,' Mother sounded a little dazed. 'I doubt it's the French this time.' She continued to look out the window. 'Mary, be a pet and go to the library. You have a better view from there. See who is ringing the bell.' She touched my arm. 'Look to Huntlaw; ten guineas to a pinch of salt that it's the great bell of Huntlaw.'

'Huntlaw!' The memories of last night flooded back. I was on my feet in an instant, knocking my chair over in my haste to run upstairs.

'Watch my furniture!' Mother called after me. 'I wish you were that eager to obey all my requests.' She lowered her voice. 'Honestly, that girl! I never know what to make of her.'

I did not care what Mother made of me. Raising my skirt, I scampered up the stairs to the library and dashed to the window. I could vaguely see the lights of Huntlaw glowing between the hills, but I could not see the bell tower with any clarity.

'Move aside, Mary.' Father adopted his most magisterial tone. I moved aside.

Opening his spyglass by the simple expedient of flicking his wrist, Father took up nearly all the space. 'Open the window for me, Mary.'

I did so as Father balanced the end of the spyglass on the lower half of the window. Mother bustled behind him, with Maggie at the rear.

'Is it Huntlaw's bell?' There was excitement in Mother's voice.

'Is it Lady Emily, Mr Hepburn? Maggie thrust forward.

'Give me space!' Father snarled. 'Agnes, please move aside a little. The rest of you, get out of my damned way!'

We moved out of Father's way. He very rarely raised his voice or swore, so we knew he must be agitated.

'It is the great bell of Huntlaw.' Father confirmed.

'Oh, dear God in his heaven.' Maggie put a hand to her young breast. 'It can't be.'

'It is,' Father handed the spyglass to Mother, who held it in both hands.

'You're right, Andrew. I can see it swaying back and forward. It's the great bell of Huntlaw.' Mother handed the spyglass to Maggie. You will notice where I was in the pecking order of Cauldneb that morning.

'I never thought I'd see the day,' Maggie said. 'My ma ayeways says to listen for the clamour of the great bell of Huntlaw.'

You will gather that I was fairly jumping up and down with frustrated excitement. 'What does it all mean?'

'Long before you were born, Mary,' Father explained, 'the Honourable Gospatrick Hume, Lady Emily's only son, vanished.'

'I know that,' I burst in.

'Very well. Lady Emily became a virtual recluse, refusing to leave her home in case she was away when her son returned home. She said that the great bell of Huntlaw, the bell that has rung to celebrate the Sabbath and warn of invasions for centuries, would be silent until the heir returned.'

'Gospatrick has come into his own,' Mother said.

Suddenly I knew what had happened. For the first time in my life, I swore. I felt the colour drain from my face.

'It's all right, Mary,' Mother ignored my language as she put her arm around my shoulders. 'Lady Emily will be pleased.'

'Who the devil is this now?' Father interrupted us. 'As if having a damned bell ring-ring-ringing all day long was not bad enough, now I have some strange horseman riding up to the door.'

I already guessed who banged at the knocker as if trying to summon the devil himself.

'Now there's an impatient fellow,' Father said as the knocker sounded again. 'Excuse me, Agnes, and you ladies. That fellow will not be bringing good news, I'll be bound. He looks too official for that.'

Leaving Mother and Maggie to study Huntlaw with the spyglass, I followed Father downstairs. My heart was pounding like the drumbeat of a marching regiment of Foot while I felt nausea rising within me. I had not recovered from the previous evening and wondered what misadventures this day would bring. Simultaneously, I wished to see my mysterious rescuer by daylight.

I waited at the curve of the stairs as the footman answered the door.

'Is your master at home?' the newcomer did not waste time in flowery speech.

'Yes, I am here,' Father advanced to meet the visitor. 'Andrew Hepburn, sir. Who are you?' Father was equally direct.

'Robert Cochrane, Messenger at Arms.' The visitor introduced himself. 'Here on the King's business.'

I looked at this vigorous man. Divested of the blackening and neckerchief, Mr Cochrane's face was strong featured, with a powerful jaw and intense grey eyes. I remembered these steady eyes from our first encounter.

'Come to my study, Mr Cochrane,' Father said. 'My man will look after your horse.' He smiled. 'You will have to forgive the uproar in the house I am afraid. We have just heard some good news about a neighbour or ours.'

Mr Cochrane nodded to me as I stepped aside to allow them passage on the stairs. 'Good morning, Miss Hepburn.'

I curtseyed. 'Good morning, Mr Cochrane.'

'I am afraid Lady Emily's news may not be as good as she hopes,' Mr Cochrane said.

Father frowned. 'Do you know what has happened?'

'I believe so,' Mr Cochrane said. 'I would like Miss Hepburn to join us.'

'Mary?' Father sounded incredulous, as well he might.

'With your permission, sir.'

'If you wish,' Father said, 'although I don't see what my daughter has to do with such matters.' He looked at me. 'Could you join us, Mary?'

'Yes, Father,' I said. So my mysterious rescuer was a Messenger at Arms. I watched his athletic form as Father opened the door of his study. Both gentlemen stepped aside to allow me to enter first. I did so, feeling like Daniel stepping into the lion's den, yet without his faith or God's grace to guide me. Sinners such as me cannot expect favour from on high.

'Take a seat, Mr Cochrane,' Father settled into his own seat behind the desk. 'Mary, you will have to stand, I'm afraid.'

'I won't hear of it,' Mr Cochrane said. 'I will not sit while a lady stands.'

'Easily remedied,' Father left the room, returning a moment later with a chair from his bedroom. 'Now we can all sit in comfort while you tell us the purpose of your visit and why my daughter should listen.'

'Miss Hepburn has her part to play,' Mr Cochrane said.

I could feel Father's gaze on me as I settled onto my chair. I said nothing.

'You will be aware what a Messenger at Arms is, Mr Hepburn,' Mr Cochrane said, 'but to make things clear for Miss Hepburn I will say, briefly, that I am an officer of the Court of Session in Edinburgh. I am responsible for serving legal documents throughout Scotland and for enforcing court orders.'

Mr Cochrane looked very efficient indeed in his grey travelling cloak and smart dark suit. 'In short, Miss Hepburn, that means I am empowered to enforce the law right across the country.'

He was older than I had at first thought, perhaps in his late thirties or early forties. Some of my interest in Mr Cochrane dwindled.

'What can I do for you, Mr Cochrane?' Father asked.

'I am aware that you had Edmund Charleton, alias Galloping Bob, alias Roaring Rab, alias Captain Ferintosh in your custody for a while,' Mr Cochrane said.

I squirmed in embarrassment while still managing to retain my silence.

'That is correct,' Father said. 'We had the fellow in Kirkton of Muirend local lockup. I had him securely chained until some blackguard picked the lock the very same night.'

'Good,' Mr Cochrane surprised us both by saying.

'Good?' Father raised his eyebrows.

'We have been chasing Charleton for months. We suspect he is guilty of many things, from highway robbery under his alias of Galloping Bob, to fraudulent theft from rich widows under the guise of Captain Ferintosh, to mere whisky smuggling as Roaring Rab.'

I listened, wondering.

'I knew he was in this area,' Mr Cochrane said, 'yet I had no proof. He is as slippery as a bucketful of eels, so we have never had sufficient to convict him.'

'Do you have sufficient now?' Father asked.

Mr Cochrane would not be rushed. 'If you had taken him to court, Mr Hepburn, I do not think you could have been successful in achieving a conviction. Besides that, I do not just want him. I also wish to apprehend his followers, including Black Jack, wanted for...' Mr Cochrane glanced at me, 'various unpleasant deeds with ladies, and Charleton's so-called wife, Isabel Snodgrass, wanted for child-stripping, child abduction, assault and other things.'

I felt my heart flutter with the memory.

Mr Cochrane continued. 'Now, I believe we may have the whole dark company. We may catch him in the midst of the most audacious crime he has yet conceived.'

'What is that, pray?' Father asked.

'Can you still hear the bell?' Mr Cochrane asked.

'I can.' Father nodded.

'That is Lady Emily celebrating that her long-lost son, Gospatrick Hume, has returned home.'

'That is what we believe,' Father said cautiously.

'It is twenty-five years since Lady Emily last saw her son. He was sixteen years old at the time. He will now be forty-one. Time will have wrought many changes on a man during that length of time.'

'That is so,' Father agreed.

'Even Lady Emily will be hard pressed to recognise him after twenty-five years.' Mr Cochrane pressed his point.

'That could be the case,' Father nodded.

'Our mutual friend, Edmund Charleton, is even as we speak, pretending to be Gospatrick Hume. He rolled up there this morning in a coach stolen from Eskbank, with Isabel Snodgrass posing as his wife and three of his followers acting as his servants.'

Father was scribbling notes as Mr Cochrane spoke. 'Are you sure of all this?'

'As sure as I can be. I have been watching this group of scoundrels for some time.'

I remained quiet.

'Can you prove that Edmund Charleton is not Gospatrick Hume?'

'I have documentary proof including signed and witnessed declarations, under oath, of the description of the man Charleton. I have prison officers' descriptions of the man Charleton including knowledge of a birthmark that I would be astonished if Gospatrick Hume shares.'

Father continued to write notes. 'I am still not sure where my daughter fits into all this.'

'I might need her as a witness,' Mr Cochrane said. 'Miss Hepburn inadvertently saw some members of the gang, possibly while she and a gentleman were exploring Wallace's Cave.'

That was delicately put, you must admit.

'A gentleman?' Father's gaze fixed on me. I could tell that he had forgotten about Captain Ferintosh in his concern for my reputation.

'Yes, father. He was one of the men who helped you round up Captain Ferintosh the other day. Alexander Colligere. You may remember that he and Mr John Aitken collided in the withdrawing room.'

'Alexander Colligere?' Father's face puckered into a frown and then nearly immediately cleared. I swear that he smiled: Alexander had that effect of people. 'Ah,' he said. 'I know the very fellow. You would be safe with him, Mary, but even so, I would be obliged if you let me know before you go gallivanting with any other gentleman, harmless or not.'

'I was not gallivanting, Father. I happened to meet him when I was perambulating around the Garleton Hills. You know how I like to go for long walks on my own.'

'I do,' Father said. 'And all that sort of thing will stop right now until I am sure that there are no more creatures like Edmund Charleton on the loose.'

'Yes, Father.' I did not argue. I could see the wisdom of Father's words and besides, the previous night had scared me more than I would ever admit. Even now I still shudder at the thought of Isabel's eyes and words.

Father nodded to me. 'We will speak more of Alexander Colligere, as you call him, Mary.'

I thought we might. 'Yes, Father.' I had escape easier than I had at first thought. That was three times Mr Cochrane had rescued me.

'In the meantime, Mr Cochrane, shall we round up these rogues?'

'We shall, Mr Hepburn.'

Father was nearly smiling as he opened the bottom drawer of his desk and produced his pistol. 'I shall send out the fiery cross.'

Sir Walter Scott's novels have made the fiery cross better known now, but back in my youth, not many people were aware of the concept. In the days of the Highland clans, if the chief wanted to raise his men, he would form a cross, dip one end in blood and set the other aflame. A runner, or a series of runners, would run around the clan territory carrying this fiery cross, which was a message for every man to gather at the clan's rendezvous spot ready for war or cattle-raid.

Now, I knew that Father did not literally mean send out a cross. He did mean to gather the local manhood to capture Captain Ferintosh for the second time.

'I'll give you a list of addresses, Cochrane.' Father said. 'I'll take the eastern half of the county if you take the western half.' He looked at me, smiling. 'It's at times like this that I wish I had a son as well as a daughter.'

'Why is that, Father?'

'To help me gather the men, Mary.'

'I can ride, Father. I know where the farms and houses are.' I lifted my chin, aware that Father was calculating how safe it would be for me. Concern, nothing else, had motivated his words to me.

'All right. Call on Elliot, Ormiston and Aitken. You've known the first two all your life. and from what I hear, you are becoming friendly with the Aitkens.'

It seemed that my parents had been discussing me. but Aitkens plural? *Was one not sufficient, or was I expected to marry a whole brood of them?* 'I'll take Coffee' I was not happy about riding to John Aitken's house.

'As long as you take care.' Father's eyes were troubled as I left the room, eager to prove myself the match for any non-existent son.

I was unsure of my feelings how I felt when I rode away from Cauldneb. It was interesting to find out that my mysterious rescuer was a court official. It had been more interesting to find out at least part of Captain Ferintosh's plan. At least I felt a little less guilty about releasing the captain from jail. And now father knew I had spoken to Alexander.

Why was that important? As I relished the feel of the wind in my face, I found myself smiling. Alexander did make me smile. I was very comfortable with him. I did not have the same feeling of excitement that Captain Ferintosh had brought. Alexander was not exciting; I could not see him riding through the night on a daring escapade. Yet, there was something about him that made me smile.

Now I was being silly. Alexander was an eccentric, a man about whom I knew next-to-nothing. *Was I grasping at straws? Yes, I was.* I was merely desperate to escape my mother's choice of a suitable husband. Alexander Colligere was not the answer. I must seek another solution. I had to persuade Mother to change her mind.

As I thought, I rode, with Coffee covering the distance at a steady pace. Mr Elliot lived furthest away, just outside Eskbank. I would call on him first, then Mr Ormiston who was inland from Prestonpans and finally with great reluctance, old Mr Aitken.

Mr Elliot was supervising his ploughmen out in the fields. He listened to my account, showed some surprise when I mentioned the Messenger at Arms and trotted back to his house. 'Pray tell your father I will be there directly,' he said as he selected a variety of weapons from his extensive armoury. Honestly, I wonder that any game birds survived with Mr Elliot on the loose. That man had more guns than Edinburgh Castle.

'Thank you, Mr Elliot.' Wheeling Coffee, I headed for Mr Ormiston's house. I must admit to feeling quite important as I pushed Coffee through the autumn-stark countryside. I was gathering men to right a wrong for which I was in part responsible. I was aiding my father. I was helping to catch a seemingly notorious rogue. And yet, within me, I retained a vestige of affection for Captain Ferintosh. Oh, I knew that he had lied to me, he had played me for the naïve fool that I had been. I was well aware of that. Yet still, I remembered his charm and poise, his elegance and those marvellously soft eyes.

Was I so shallow as to fall for appearances and smooth words rather than the solid decency of a man like, say, Mr Cochrane? Or even John Aitken?

I turned from that thought with quick alarm. John Aitken was far too old. But Mr Cochrane now, a man of proven resource, a man of position who had shown himself a gentleman of the first order; could I consider him?

'Halloa!' The voice challenged me. I had been riding automatically as my mind raced along different lines. 'Where are you off to, young lady?'

'Mr Ormiston's house of Garvalton,' I replied, reining up.

'Garvalton is just over the rise there.' A group of farm servants were having a break from ploughing the rich red earth, chewing mightily on hunks of salmon. 'He's at home, I believe.'

'Thank you.' I knew the way already. Lifting a hand in acknowledgement, I turned Coffee off the road and onto the drive to Mr Ormiston's house.

Mr Ormiston was on all fours in his front room, with two little girls riding on his back. He looked up with a broad smile. 'Miss Hepburn! You have caught me at somewhat of a disadvantage, I fear.'

'I am sorry to disturb you, Mr Ormiston,' I removed Father's hat that I had quite taken to wearing. I told Mr Ormiston the story as his wife came close to listen.

'Does Mr Hepburn desperately require my husband?' Mrs Ormiston was a plump, matronly woman with rough red cheeks, and a small child balanced on her hip.

'I must do my duty, my dear.' Mr Ormiston stood, holding a child in each arm. 'Miss Hepburn, pray tell your father I will be there at once.'

'Thank you, Mr Ormiston.' Leaving the domestic bliss of Garvalton, I was back on Coffee in minutes, kicking in my heels as I headed for John Aitken's house.

Once again, my feelings were mixed as I rode to my final destination. I was tired now, with Coffee flagging beneath me. By the time I approached Mr Aitken's house of Tyneford all the excitement of carrying news had worn off. I could feel the weariness heavy on my shoulders.

I had never visited Tyneford before although I must have passed the property a hundred times on my various perambulations. As the name suggests, it was situated on a ford of the River Tyne that wends its way through the Lothian countryside. With all the troubles of English border raiders in the bad old days, the local knight had built a tower house to guard the crossing. Now the tower had been added to and extended to form a substantial Adam-style building, too large to be a mere farmhouse, yet not sufficiently grandiose to be termed a mansion.

I halted Coffee on the outskirts of the policies, looking over this house that would be my home if I married John Aitken. It was undoubtedly larger than Cauldneb, more pretentious and with the sunlight reflecting on an array of windows, Mr Aitken evidently had a sufficiently large fortune not to be concerned about the window tax. There was wealth in Tyneford.

'Are you looking for the master?' The man must have been the gamekeeper, a broad-shouldered, red-faced individual with a fowling piece carried in the crook of his arm.

'I am looking for Mr John Aitken,' I said.

The gamekeeper pointed to a stable block at the side of the house. 'Try in there, Miss. He's a right one for the horses is Mr Aitken.'

The gamekeeper had been correct. Mr Aitken emerged at the sound of Coffee's hooves. 'Bless you, Miss Hepburn! You look as if you're all done in!'

'Good morning, Mr Aitken,' I said, stiffly formal. 'I have a message from my father.'

'It can wait,' Mr Aitken said. 'I have a message for you. Dismount from that horse and get some sustenance. God bless you, lassie, you look as if you've ridden for hours! Dismount, my dear girl, before you fall off.'

I was not loath to obey, sliding off Coffee onto the ground with Mr Aitken's hands guiding me down. Still tired from my exertions of the previous night, the bruises that Isabel Snodgrass had given me were also aching abominably.

'Now come inside and get something to eat.' Mr Aitken's voice was benign. 'My stable lads will care for your horse. Coffee isn't she?'

'Yes. Coffee.'

Strangely, given my previous thoughts about Mr Aitken, I was quite grateful for his help. His words were kindly as he brought me inside the drawing room, despite my sweat-froth- and-mud spattered clothes. Riding muddy tracks in a Scottish autumn is not the cleanest of occupations.

'Mrs Mackay!' When Mr Aitken lifted his voice, a middle-aged woman appeared. 'Mrs Mackay, this is Miss Mary Hepburn, the young lady from Cauldneb of whom we have often spoken.'

'So I see, sir,' Mrs Mackay ran an assessing gaze over me. 'She's been riding hard by the look of it.'

'I would say so, Mrs Mackay. I think a dish of tea is in order.'

'I would recommend something more filling sir. How about vegetable broth, Miss Hepburn, with a good chunk of bread and cheese? There's nothing more filling on a chill day.'

'Oh, thank you, Mrs Mackay.' I had not expected such a cordial welcome at Tyneford.

Mr Aitken took my cloak and hat. 'Now sit you down Miss Hepburn. While Mrs Mackay works her magic, you can tell me what brings you here in such a lather.'

I must admit to feeling quite faint as I sat on Mr Aitken's best armchair while he perched on a creepie stool at my side. I took the opportunity to look around the room, wondering what sort of house Mr Aitken ran. Comfortable rather than luxurious, there were shelves of books in one corner, and a glass case showing various botanical specimens in another. Mr Aitken had literary and scientific tastes then. That was all in his favour.

'Now Miss Hepburn,' Mr Aitken was all attention as he sat at my feet. 'Pray tell me what your father's message is. It must be urgent for you to ride so fast.'

'It is, sir,' I related the events of the morning as Mr Aitken listened, nodding at all the correct places.

'I see. This Cochrane fellow, did he say how he got his information?'

'He said that he has been hunting for Edmund Charleton, Captain Ferintosh, for months, Mr Aitken.'

'Very well.' Mr Aitken stood up. 'I will repair to Cauldneb immediately.'

I made to rise.

'No, no, my dear Miss Hepburn.' Mr Aitken put a light hand on my shoulder. 'You have done your duty admirably. There is no urgency for you to leave. You may stay here as long as you wish. Recover your strength, taste Mrs Mackay's good cooking, look around the house.' His smile took ten years off his age. 'Make yourself at home. Meanwhile, I will ride to Cauldneb.'

Make myself at home. With Mrs Mackay fussing over me like a cow over her calf and the fire sparking brightly in the grate, it certainly felt homely in that front room of Tyneford House.

Dressed for the journey, Mr Aitken glanced in before he left. 'Don't you leave here until you are rested and ready, Miss Hepburn.' He smiled, pointing his riding whip at Mrs Mackay. 'Mrs Mackay will look after you as she has been looking after me and mine for years!'

'Please call me Mary,' I don't know why I said that. 'My given name is Mary.'

Mr Aitken's eyes softened. 'Thank you.' He hesitated. 'Thank you, Mary.' I thought he was going to ask me to call him John. Instead, he gave a little bow and backed out of the room. A few moments later I heard the drumbeat of hooves.

I sighed.

'Eat your soup,' Mrs Mackay stood silently in the corner. 'Or should that be drink your soup?' She smiled. 'I am never sure.'

I ate, or perhaps drunk, my soup.

'You are troubled, Miss Hepburn, if you don't mind me saying.'

Mother was always telling me that I allowed servants to be too familiar with me. 'Do I appear troubled?'

'Yes,' Mrs Mackay watched as I ate. 'You were watching Mr Aitken as if you were afraid of him.'

I stopped with the spoon halfway to my mouth. 'I am not afraid of Mr Aitken, Mrs Mackay.'

'You will have no need to be,' Mrs Mackay said. 'If you ignore his occasional gruffness you will find he is a very benevolent gentleman.'
I replaced the spoon in my plate. 'Do you know Mr Aitken well?'
'I've been his housekeeper for upwards of twenty years.' Mrs Mackay said.

That was another of Mother's sayings. *You can tell a family by their servants.* If the servants remain, then the family is composed of respectable people. If the servants continuously change, then avoid them. I was beginning to get the measure of gruff Mr John Aitken.

'Thank you.' I continued with the soup. It was excellent; every bit as good as anything that our cook made.

'If you permit me to say, Miss Hepburn,' Mrs Mackay said. 'I heard a rumour that you may be joining this family at some time in the future?'

The words jolted me. Was everybody determined to marry me off to John Aitken? 'Have you been talking to my mother?' I could not keep the edge from my voice.

'Your mother? God bless you no, Miss Hepburn! It was Mr John who mentioned the possibility.'

I was unsure what to say. Had my mother and Mr Aitken made all the arrangements already? Was the whole deal so complete that Mr Aitken could even tell his servants? I ate the soup automatically, wondering why Mr Aitken had not even mentioned the possibility of marriage when he was with me.

When I looked up, Mrs Mackay had left the room. Despite the confusion in my mind, my curiosity still compelled me to examine the books in the room. If you are a book-person, then you will understand.

I am not sure what I had expected, perhaps farming tomes or works of classical authors, so I was surprised to find books on botany, biology and horticulture. Clearly, Mr Aitken was a man who hid his interests as well as a kind nature. There were also maps of far-flung places, with a book of sailing directions, which intrigued me. Hidden among the books was very battered copy of *The Odyssey*, which is undoubtedly my favourite book of all time. Unable to resist the temptation, I lifted it and thumbed through the pages. The familiar words weaved their spell on me as my opinion of Mr John Aitken rose a notch higher. *If only he were not so old!*

I left the withdrawing room in a thoughtful frame of mind. It seemed that everybody who mattered expected me to marry John Aitken. My opinion was neither sought nor considered. Yet there was much to be said in favour of that gruffly amiable old man.

Mr Aitken's stable lads had cared well for Coffee. She had been washed, groomed and fed. They grinned as I entered the stable. 'There you are, Miss Hepburn,' one freckle-faced youth said. 'All ready for you!'

'Thank you,' I recognised a lad who loved his job. Such servants are a blessing and a boon.

After a few moments waiting for the lads to replace Coffee's saddle, I mounted and moved off again. With my messages delivered, I had no need to hurry. I ambled across country, nearly nodding off in the saddle until I entered an ancient copse near Hailes Castle and nearly trampled on a man lying on his face to examine something on the ground.

'Whoa there!' I sawed at the reins to halt Coffee. The horse reared up, her hooves missing the man by a few inches. 'What the devil are you doing?' I allowed my temper full rein after holding it in check ever since Mrs Mackay's confirmation of my apparent impending marriage. 'I could have killed you!'

Alexander Colligere did not move. 'Look at what I have here. I didn't know it spread to this part of the world.'

As always with that man, I could not help smiling and shaking my head. 'Did you hear what I said? I said I could have killed you!'

'Yes, I heard you. I'm glad you didn't.' Alexander twisted to lie on his back. 'What are you doing out here?'

'My father is gathering the clans again.'

Alexander rose to his feet. 'I'd better go along and do my bit for king and country.' He was taller than I remembered, I thought absently. 'Are you heading for Cauldneb, Mary?'

'Yes.' My smile faded as I remembered how serious the situation was. 'You may be too late to help.'

'In that case, I had better hurry,' Alexander looked around. 'I left my horse somewhere.'

'He's tied to that tree,' I saw a pale gelding grazing at the side of the wood.

'Come on Masson.' Alexander untied his horse, blowing in his nostrils and offering a carrot. 'I named him after Francis Masson,' he said. 'You'll have heard of him?'

I had not.

'He's a plant hunter,' Alexander said, which meant nothing to me. He mounted Masson with surprisingly easy grace. 'Are you coming?'

For some reason, I wanted to show this man that I could ride as well as he and kicked Coffee into a trot. When Alexander responded, we hurried along the road side by side, throwing up showers of mud as we grinned at each other.

With two of us in competition, the miles passed quickly. Even so, I was flagging by the time we reached home.

'I wondered when you would return,' Mother was at the stone pillars that marked the gate of Cauldneb. 'And you have company, I see.'

'You'll remember Mr Alexander Colligere,' I said.

'Mr...' Mother looked confused for a moment. I had noticed that people tended to forget about Alexander. I presumed that was because he was a little out of the ordinary. 'Oh, yes. I remember this gentleman.'

'Are we too late? Mr Colligere wishes to help father.'

'Mr Ormiston, Mr Elliot and Mr Aitken,' Mother glance at Alexander when she said the last name, 'rode out with your father and some other men some hour and a half ago. I doubt you will catch them now, Mr...'

'Masson is a fast horse,' Alexander said. 'Lady Emily's house of Huntlaw is it not?' He pulled at the reins.

I hated to see Alexander ride away alone. He would probably get distracted by an oak tree or a clump of nettles or some such. 'Wait. I'll come with you!' I followed, ignoring Mother's shout to come back.

It was only a half-hour minute ride to Huntlaw, even with a rather tired Coffee. Alexander made it into a bit of a race, nearly steeple chasing his way across the countryside in a manner that, frankly, I had not thought him capable of. He only slowed down when Mr Ormiston rode into our path, a short distance from Huntlaw.

'Where are you two going?' Mr Ormiston asked.

'We're going to help Father,' I said.

Mr Ormiston frowned. 'Maybe Colligere is, Miss Hepburn, but this is no place for a young lady. It could be dangerous. These are desperate people in there.'

'It's no more dangerous for me than it is for a man,' I said, stupidly. Of course, I knew that women were not as strong as men, or as skilled with weapons. All the same, I was too inquisitive to be left out.

'Ormiston is right,' Alexander betrayed me, the pig. 'I should never have taken you here.'

'You did not take me. I came of my own accord.' I faced him, with my hot temper rising once more.

'Enough, you two.' Mr Ormiston said. 'Miss Hepburn, you can be usefully employed if you relieve me here. If any more gentlemen arrive, send them on to Mr Hepburn. He is gathering his men behind the old stables.'

'Thank you, Mr Ormiston.' I realised that I was only at the very fringe of things, but rather that than not being involved at all. 'What is happening?'

Mr Hepburn, your father, and that King's Messenger fellow, Cochrane, are organising all the gentlemen who arrive,' Mr Ormiston said. 'As far as I know, the idea is to form a cordon around Huntlaw so nobody can escape, then Hepburn, I beg your pardon, Mr Hepburn, Cochrane and a few others will move in to challenge this Charleton fellow.'

'Poor Lady Emily won't be pleased to find that Charleton is a charlatan,' Alexander said.

'Oh, clever,' I acknowledged his play on words.

'You stay here, Miss Hepburn if you please,' Mr Ormiston said. 'Direct any late coming gentlemen to the old stables. 'You ride with me, Colligere.'

Alexander threw me a wink as he turned. For some reason that I did not understand, he took hold of my arm. 'Look after yourself' he said, urgently. 'If there is any trouble, keep well out of the way, won't you? I don't wish you of all people to get hurt.'

Me of all people? What on earth did he mean by that? I watched the pair of them ride into the shelter belt of woodland around the policies of Huntlaw, pulled father's hat firmly down over my head and waited for events.

And waited.

And waited.

And waited.

As I may have indicated elsewhere, I am not the most patient of women.

Time passed without anything seeming to happen. I dismounted from poor Coffee and patted her. 'You've had a long day, Coffee,' I said, as she nuzzled my face. 'You'll be home soon, I hope, for a long rest in your stable.'

The short day was beginning to fade into the late autumn evening in which everything seems so melancholic. There was no wind and only a solitary bird, who's cheeping only enhanced the loneliness. I thought of poor Lady Emily waiting day after day, year after year, for her long-lost son to come home, only to be fooled by Captain Ferintosh.

'Mary,' Alexander appeared at my side. 'Your father needs you.' With Alexander, there was never any formality. I did not mind. It was a refreshing change to speak openly.

'Why?'

'You are the only person who has seen Edmund Charleton's men close to. They might hide among Lady Emily's servants.'

Although I was keen to be active in helping, I had to speak my mind. 'Surely Lady Emily will be able to recognise strangers.'

'Lady Emily has been alone for over twenty years. Who knows what or who she can or cannot recognise?'

'Come on then, Alexander,' I mounted and led the way, with Alexander's Masson a neck behind me.

There were more than a dozen men alongside Father when he rode to greet me. 'I am not happy about you being here,' he said.

'I wish to be useful,' I said.

'Stay in the background and if there is any trouble, run outside until I say it is safe.'

'Yes, Father.' That was good advice. I had no intention of meeting Isabel Snodgrass again.

'Ready, lads?'

I had never seen Father at this sort of work before. He was very efficient, ordering three riders to the back of the house and four others to patrol the sides in case any of the culprits escaped out of a window.

'On the count of three.' Father dismounted, ordered one of the younger men to care for the horses and advanced to the front door of the house. I had expected him to knock politely, but he pushed in without hesitation.

I was equally surprised to see Alexander only a few steps behind father, with Cochrane and Ormiston close by. I hurried forward until John Aitken put a large hand on my arm.

'You stay with me, Miss Hepburn.' He winked at me. '*Mary*. We'll leave the rough stuff to the young men and those who are paid for such endeavours.'

'Father...'

'Your father knows what he is doing.'

I was not sure what to think. I did know that I felt perfectly safe with this grumpy old man looking after me.

'Lady Emily!' Mr Cochrane roared the name. 'I am Robert Cochrane, Messenger at Arms.'

Naturally, the noise we made attracted the servants, who crowded into the hall. There were far fewer than I expected, only three for a house this size. Lady Emily arrived, dressed in more formal wear than was normal for a woman in her own home, with a huge turban on her head and a black frown on her wrinkled face.

'What's the meaning of this?' Lady Emily goggled at Mr Cochrane. 'Who are all these people in my house? James! Throw them out!'

James proved to be her butler, a man who must have been in his late sixties or even seventies. He stepped forward bravely, prepared to do his duty.

'Lady Emily.' Although Mr Cochrane spoke quietly, there was no doubting his authority. 'I am Robert Cochrane, a Messenger at Arms. I beg of you to listen to what I have to say.'

'I will not listen to you. My son has just come home.' Lady Emily raised her voice. 'Gospatrick! Gospatrick! Come and throw these people out of our house.'

I was not surprised when Gospatrick Hume, alias Captain Ferintosh, alias Edmund Charleton, alias Uncle Tom Cobley and all, I should not wonder, did not appear.

'Gospatrick!' Lady Emily said again. 'Where are you?'

'Lady Emily,' Mr Cochrane said again, every bit as quietly. 'I beg you to listen to me.'

'I've nothing to say to you.' Lady Emily barely looked at Mr Cochrane. 'Gospatrick! Gospatrick! Where is that boy?'

'The gentleman you seek is not your son, my Lady,' Mr Cochrane said. 'He is an imposter.'

'I know my own son,' Lady Emily said.

'I'm afraid your son is dead, My Lady.'

I do not know what I had expected when I entered Huntlaw House. I had not expected Mr Cochrane to make such a brutally dramatic announcement.

'My son... Gospatrick?' For an instant, I saw sanity in Lady Emily's faded eyes.

'I am sorry to have to break the news.' Mr Cochrane took Lady Emily's arm and guided her to a long oaken settle that sat beneath an array of portraits in the grand hall. 'The Honourable Gospatrick Hume joined the East India Company as a clerk. He died of fever in Bengal seventeen years ago. I do have documentary proof.'

'Oh.' Lady Emily slumped on the settle for a long minute. I was sure I saw tears in her eyes, but then she straightened her back. The Scottish nobility do not reveal their emotions in public, however heart-rending the news. 'The line has not ended. The property will fall to my second nephew. The name will continue.'

Mr Cochrane nodded. 'I believe that is so, Your Ladyship.'

Lady Emily stood up, all traces of grief removed from her face. 'So be it. Where is the imposter who dared take my family name?'

'We are searching for him, your Ladyship.' Father spoke quietly. 'We will bring the rogue to justice.'

Sudden noises behind the house indicated that the search had been successful. 'Come this way, gentlemen.' Lady Emily gave me a brief nod. 'And you, Miss Hepburn.'

'Do you know who I am?'

'You are Miss Mary Hepburn of Cauldneb. Come along.'

My crazy old lady had proved to be less mad than I thought. People are seldom what they appear, in my opinion, and we have a habit of applying false, and often derogatory, labels to those we scarcely know. We do like to categorise our neighbours so we can store them in compartments within our minds. As will be evident from my own story, we are often well wide of the truth.

Moving with surprising speed for an elderly woman, Lady Emily guided us through her home. I had expected a mausoleum with empty or dusty rooms. The place was pristine. Lady Emily was anything but crazy. In nautical terms, she ran a tight ship.

The sound of voices increased as we drew nearer to the rear of the house.

'Excuse me, ladies,' Mr Aitken gave a brief bow. 'Duty calls.' He ran ahead, as eager as a young man in his prime.

We emerged from the back door to see Mr Ormiston and Mr Aitken struggling with three men. One man had his hands around the throat of John Aitken, while Mr Ormiston had one on the ground. The third was Captain Ferintosh. Without hesitation, Mr Cochrane and Alexander dashed forward.

'Be careful, Alexander,' I warned.

As Mr Cochrane leapt to help Mr Ormiston, Alexander banged into the man who held Mr Aitken. Now, I am no expert at describing scenes of mayhem, so suffice to say that between them, Alexander and Mr Aitken succeeded in overpowering their adversary. As Mr Aitken sat on him, Alexander produced a length of cord from his pocket and tied the fellow up. That man seemed to carry everything with him except a horse and carriage.

In the meantime, Mr Cochrane had disabled another man with a most effective punch. After a lingering look at me, Captain Ferintosh fled into the woods of Huntlaw policies.

'There are two more men in the gang.' As you may imagine, I was wild with excitement at all these goings-on. 'One is called Jack Samson. There is also a woman called Isabel Snodgrass.' I do not know why I mentioned the woman's name, but it seemed important to do so.

'Are you all right, Miss Hepburn?' Mr Aitken looked directly at me. 'You should not be involved in this squabbling. I'm surprised at you, Cochrane, allowing such a thing! And I am even more surprised at you!' Mr Aitken prodded Alexander in the ribs.

'I could not leave her outside,' Alexander held out a hand as if to touch me.

'Miss Hepburn is unharmed,' Lady Emily stood at my side. 'You gentlemen still have work to do.'

'Catch Charleton,' Mr Cochrane ordered. 'I want the head and the body of the snake. I don't want anybody to come back to the house until Charleton and Snodgrass are in custody.' He turned to me. 'Miss Hepburn. Can you say with certainty that these two fellows were part of Charleton's gang?'

Mr Cochrane pulled his prisoners to their feet by the simple expedient of grabbing them by the hair and yanking hard. I stared at the contorted, now mud-smeared faces. 'Yes,' I said.

'Good.' Mr Cochrane nodded, 'Mr Aitken, could you put them somewhere safe? And you, Miss Hepburn, remain in the house if you please. This is no job for a lady.'

'Miss Hepburn will remain with me,' Lady Emily said. 'Come, Miss Hepburn. Leave the men to do their work.'

After years of thinking of Lady Emily as an eccentric old lady, now I sat opposite her as we drank tea, ate the most delicious scones imaginable and watched as the men spread out to scour the woodland.

'I'm sorry to hear about your son,' I said.

'Thank you.' Lady Emily bit delicately into a scone. 'He chose his path. Men do that.'

'So it seems,' I said.

'That man Edmund Charleton; he has chosen a different path, one that will invariably lead to the gallows.' Lady Emily sighed. 'It is such a pity. He is a handsome fellow with such impeccable manners. It's hard to believe that a man with the pretensions of a gentleman could be a wrong 'un.'

I nodded. 'I liked the fellow, your Ladyship.'

'So did I,' Lady Emily said. 'He did remind me of Gospatrick. He gave me a few hours of such intense pleasure when I thought Gospatrick had returned.' She looked at me from her ancient, rheumy eyes. 'You must think me such a fool to believe that such a man could be my son.'

I shook my head. 'Not at all, your Ladyship. Captain Ferintosh, or Edmund Charleton or whatever name he chooses to call himself, is a most accomplished actor. He should be on stage.'

'I feel such a fool.'

'You're not.' I wondered what the protocol was for a woman such as me consoling an elderly Lady. I sighed; after the past few days, I did not really care. Leaning forward, I patted Lady Emily's arm. 'You're a very sensible lady.'

That sounded far more condescending than I had intended. I sat back, expecting to feel the full wrath of an insulted aristocrat. Lady Emily only smiled.

'Your husband will be happy to know you are safe.'

'I don't have a husband,' I said.

It was Lady Emily's turn to pat my arm. 'You have, Miss Hepburn, in all but name. I saw the way that man looked at you. He was not concerned about any old gentlewoman.' Lady Emily gave a throaty chuckle. 'He had very tender eyes for you.'

That man could only mean Mr Aitken when he had rebuked Mr Cochrane and Alexander for allowing me to come here. Once again I had pushed the thought of my impending engagement to John Aitken to the back of my mind. Now it emerged again in all its depressing reality.

'My Lady.' The voice came from behind me.

Captain Ferintosh emerged from behind a curtain with a pistol in his hand. 'I think we have unfinished business, Lady Emily, and you, Miss Hepburn.'

Chapter Fourteen

I rose, prepared to fight but not knowing how to begin. In a lonely childhood bereft of brothers and sisters, one does not gain the necessary skills required to challenge a man with a pistol. Oh, I tried. I threw myself forward as women do in all the worst romances, and got a hefty slap on the jaw for my pains. I sprawled on the floor in an undignified heap.

'Get up,' Isabel joined Captain Ferintosh. She kicked me, as she had done before. 'Get up!' She called me some foul names that I will not sully this page by using.

Jack was also there, looking a trifle concerned as he took Lady Emily by the arm.

'Let go of me!' Lady Emily's attempted slap was no more effective than my lunge had been. Neither of us gave much resistance as Captain Ferintosh rounded us up like cattle. 'You are our way out,' Captain Ferintosh said.

I tried another tactic. 'Captain, for the sake of old times, you could let us go.'

'There were no old times,' Isabel emphasised her words by another vicious kick. Honestly, that woman was a devil with her feet. 'Now move, or I'll set about you.'

I had learned not to like Captain Ferintosh or Jack, but it was Isabel who scared me the most. Although the captain was the nominal leader,

I genuinely believe that Isabel was the driving force of that unpleasant little group.

'You spoiled my plans,' Isabel confirmed my suspicions with her next words. 'We were going to act as Lady and Lord of the manor. We were going to use this house as our base for a company that would control whisky distilling in southern Scotland.'

'So that was why Captain Ferintosh attacked Simmy and Peter,' I said. 'Not to help me! He was getting rid of the opposition.'

'That's right, my little lady!' Isabel's face twisted with hatred when she glared at me. 'You think you are so important. Edmund was only getting information from you, you little...' she repeated her earlier obscenities. 'Now,' Isabel poked a hard finger into Lady Emily's ribs. 'Her Ladyship here will show us her best treasures. We'll rob this place inside out.'

'I'll show you nothing,' Lady Emily lifted her determined old chin. 'We won't help you one iota.'

It may have been flattering for Lady Emily to include me in her defiance, but it was also a little bit frightening.

'You old crow!' Isabel responded with insults and a back-handed slap that threw Lady Emily to the ground. 'I'll teach you!'

'You leave her alone!' I tried to intervene as Isabel landed a couple of hefty kicks on Lady Emily's hip and thigh. Inevitably, Isabel turned her attention to me.

'Enough!' Captain Ferintosh snapped. 'We don't have the time for this. You can have them both later.'

I did not find Captain Ferintosh's words very reassuring as I picked myself up and helped Lady Emily to her feet.

'Come on, your Ladyship,' I said. 'We'll get out of this, don't you fear.'

'We'll take what we can find,' Captain Ferintosh said, 'throw it in the coach and run. With these two as hostages, Cochrane and Hepburn won't dare pursue us.'

Ferintosh led us through the house, grabbing any object he thought might be valuable. As thieves go, he was thoroughly unprofessional, while Isabel, for all her violence, knew nothing about art or silverware. Ignoring a beautiful portrait by Alan Ramsay, they stole cheap prints that would not fetch a guinea in any decent art shop. Opening drawers they grabbed handfuls of gold-plated cutlery, leaving those of solid silver and three times the value; breaking a glass cabinet, they lifted Indian brassware in the mistaken belief they were made of gold.

After our crazy careen through the house, Captain Ferintosh halted at one of the side doors. 'Jack: look out the window. See if Cochrane or his boys are about.'

Jack returned a minute later. 'The coast is clear,' he used the old smuggling term.

'Go and get the coach,' Captain Ferintosh ordered. 'We're right opposite the stables.'

'How about Wullie and Tam?'

'Leave them. All the more pickings for us.' Isabel decided, proving to me that there was no honour among thieves.

If ever a woman needed a white knight to ride up and rescue her, it was me at that minute. If Captain Ferintosh and especially Isabel retained us as captives, I could not see any brightness in our future.

If I were alone, I would have lifted my skirts and ran. I was as fit as any woman, and I would have defied Isabel to catch me, or Captain Ferintosh to shoot me. Pistols are notoriously inaccurate at anything except very close range. I also suspected that, for all his words, the captain had some affection for me. His initial hesitation would enable me to increase the distance. However, I was not alone. I refused to even contemplate leaving Lady Emily with these three blackguards.

I did have one weapon, a woman's last line of defence. Immediately that Jack opened the door I opened my mouth and screamed as loudly as I could. It was the first time in my life I had ever done that. Screaming was not allowed in Cauldneb. The Lord only knows what my mother would have done if I had ever acted in such a manner.

As it as I only had time for one full-blooded scream before Captain Ferintosh clamped his hand across my mouth, while Isabel, predictably gave me a hefty kick. As I winced under Isabel's boot, I hoped that my single scream had been sufficient.

It appeared not. There was no clatter of hooves, no white knight in shining armour galloping to our rescue. Captain Ferintosh held me tight as Isabel continued with her kicking practice while Jack scrabbled across the cobbled courtyard to fetch the coach. The rain had increased to a downpour that bounced from the ground. Miniature waterfalls wept from the guttering.

I struggled in the captain's grip, tried to bite his fingers and kicked back at Isabel, all with an equal lack of success.

Either the horses were still standing in their traces, or Jack was a highly skilled coachman, for the coach rumbled out of the coach-house within minutes. Shortly before, I had been hoping for a white knight. Now he appeared. I had thought that the eminently capable Mr Cochrane would have acted as Sir Lancelot, however, it was the unlikely figure of Alexander who raced around the corner.

'Who is that damned lunatic,' Captain Ferintosh said as Alexander pranced in front of the horses, waving both hands in the air.

I felt my heart-beat increase, for the Lord knew that Alexander was a decent fellow, but hardly Sir Lancelot. Even so, his capering halted the horses, one of which reared up while the other turned aside.

'Mary!' Rather than run to me, Alexander pulled open the door of the coach and peered inside. 'Are you in there?' That was all the time it took for Jack to get the horses back under control.

'Over here!' I tried to shout, but with the captain's hand over my mouth, all I could manage was a stifled squawk.

Not so her Ladyship. For all her advanced years, Lady Emily possessed a splendid pair of lungs, which she now put to good use in a mighty, a tremendous scream. If ever prizes were given for loud, ear-shaking screams, Lady Emily's would win accolades wherever screams are honoured.

Alexander turned around in an instant, only for Jack to slam into him in a charge that must have shaken every bone in his body. I fully expected my poor plant collector to fold under the impact. He did not.

Thrust back against the wheel of the coach; he abruptly lifted his knee to catch Jack in a most personal place. As Jack doubled up, gasping, Alexander ran towards the open door.

Captain Ferintosh released me to grab at the pistol that he had thrust through the waistband of his breeches.

I can still picture that scene in vivid detail. I saw Alexander running with his hat fallen off to roll on the ground, his mouth open and hands closed into fists. I saw Captain Ferintosh hauling at his pistol, his oh-so-handsome face contorted into a snarl. I saw Lady Emily gamely trying to wrestle with Isobel, who was a full head taller and bigger in every way. Only then did I realise that everybody had forgotten about me in this mad escapade. Without thinking, I barged into Captain Ferintosh, unbalancing him so when he fired, his shot flew well wide of anybody. The captain lashed out at me with his pistol, missing when Alexander grabbed hold of his arm.

I joined in the melee, with all five of us wrestling in a quite undignified, if very exciting, manner. The opposition was beginning to get the upper hand when Mr John Aitken arrived, panting like a dog in midsummer, with my father at his heels.

'Mary!' One-handed as he was, Father lifted Captain Ferintosh from me and threw him against the wall, where John Aitken held him secure with his forearm across the captain's throat. 'Are you injured?'

'Only a couple of bruises,' I said. 'Nothing that won't heal.'

'Your Ladyship!' Father turned his attention to Lady Emily, who Alexander and Mr Ormiston had released from the furiously-struggling Isobel. 'Are you hurt, your Ladyship?'

'Not in the slightest,' that indomitable lady replied. 'I rather enjoyed that little encounter. This woman requires a sharp lesson in manners!' Lady Emily scowled at Isobel. 'Her language would defile the gutter.'

I leaned against the wall, careless of the rain that continued to thunder down. 'Thank you, gentlemen.'

'I heard you yell,' Alexander said. 'I knew it was you.' Sodden after spending two hours scouring Lady Emily's policies for Captain Ferintosh, he shook some of the rainwater from his hair.

'Did you get them all? Well done!' Mr Cochrane arrived, all efficiency and bustle. 'Well, Mr Hepburn, it looks like Charleton and all the gang are in custody.'

'It looks like it,' Father said. For a moment we stood in the teeming rain, gasping for breath.

'You will recall that Charleton escaped from the local lock-up last time,' Mr Cochrane said.

'That is correct,' Father looked uncomfortable at the reminder.

'I think we'd be best taking the whole lot to the jail in Haddington,' Mr Cochrane said. 'We can do all the paperwork there.' He looked around. 'We don't need everybody to come. Miss Hepburn, you can come along. Lady Emily, there is no need for both of you.'

'I'm not staying behind,' Lady Emily said. 'That Snodgrass woman swore at me. I want to see her locked up.'

'As you wish your Ladyship,' Mr Cochrane said. 'In that case, Miss Hepburn, there is no need for *you* to come along. I'll need you, Mr Hepburn, of course, with Mr Ormiston and Mr Aitken. The rest of you, thank you for your assistance. You may return to your homes. I will send an officer around for your depositions during the next few days.'

'You're soaking wet,' Father said to me. 'You'd better get home and change as quickly as you can.' He raised his voice. 'Lady Emily! Remember to lock the doors!'

I stood in the rain, watching as Father and Mr Cochrane ordered their now manacled prisoners across the courtyard.

'Come on!' Lady Emily encouraged them with a riding whip, landing stinging blows on Isabel. 'You foul-mouthed harridan! You kicked me, you viper!'

'More power to your arm, your Ladyship.' I watched Isabel jump when the lash cracked across her prominent behind.

'I can do this all day,' Lady Emily said, striking again. 'Go on; get into the coach!'

'You can get yourself home now, Mary.' Alexander was not in the least interested in Lady Emily's antics.

'There is no rush.' I watched with considerable satisfaction as Lady Emily continued to gain her revenge on Isabel.

'No,' Alexander said. 'There is no rush. However, I do think we'd be better out of the rain.'

'Yes.' I waited until the entertainment had finished and both coaches rolled away, the prisoners in front and Her Ladyship following behind, as an escort, no doubt.

For some reason, I felt quite melancholic that the Captain Ferintosh episode had finished. I doubted that I would ever experience anything so exciting again. My future life as wife to Mr John Aitken would be achingly dull in comparison. When I returned to Cauldneb, this period would be in the past. I felt too young to enter my decades of dullness.

'Let's go into the house,' I said. 'Lady Emily won't mind.'

'The servants locked the doors before they took her away in the coach,' Alexander said. 'There are stables.'

'A stable it must be,' I said.

I was glad not to go home yet and glad I had such comfortable company with which to spend my time. As the excitement of the day wore off, I felt momentarily dispirited, and then another, more unfamiliar excitement took over. I could not identify it, although I recognised that it was even more significant than the fleeting adventure of knowing Captain Ferintosh.

Shaking my head and telling myself not to be foolish, I followed Alexander into the stable as the rain hammered down upon us.

Chapter Fifteen

'It's drier in here,' Alexander said.

We looked out at the teeming rain, looked at each other and sat down on bales of straw.

'We have a choice,' Alexander said.

'We have,' I moved aside to dodge a persistent drip that came through the roof.

Alexander nodded. 'Yes, Mary. You'd better move before you get wet.'

I looked at the puddle forming around my feet. 'I think it's a bit late for that.' We laughed together. 'Look at the pair of us. We're like a pair of drowned rats. Tell me your choice, Alexander.'

'We can stay here until the rain moderates,' Alexander said, 'or we can ride through the storm.'

I looked out of the half-open door. The rain was bouncing from the quickly spreading puddles. Ahead, the clouds concealed Lammermuir, with tendrils of grey probing into the lower ground.

'We're already wet,' I said. 'We can't get much wetter riding home.'

'Are you in a hurry?' Alexander stood up and walked to the door, leaving a trail of wet footprints. 'I'm not.'

I did not wish to admit that I felt very relaxed in Alexander's company. After all the recent excitements, it felt good to sit, do nothing and feel safe. I looked up suddenly. That was true; I did feel safe with this man.

'If we sit here like this we'll both end up with a fever.' My words contradicted my desires. 'We'd better get home and into dry clothes.'

'Why not dry our clothes here?'

'We'll need a fire for that,' I did not object. I had no desire to ride a wet horse through pelting rain. Also, and probably very selfishly, I wanted to find out more about Alexander. I found him endlessly, refreshingly intriguing.

'That is not a problem.' Alexander said. 'There are stone slabs on the ground and plenty straw and lumber.'

'We have no flame,' I pointed out helpfully. 'You don't smoke so you won't have a flint.'

Alexander smiled. 'Now how do you know I don't smoke? Have you been spying on me?'

'I happened to notice,' I said.

'I do have a flint,' Alexander said. 'Fire is useful when I stay out overnight.'

'You stay out overnight?'

'I prefer the outdoors to the indoors. Let's get the fire going first.' Alexander's smile widened. 'I've done this before. We'll have to make space to ensure the fire does not spread.'

We worked together, pushing back the bales of hay from the slabs. We also brushed away any loose straw so that sparks could not ignite something we could not control. I watched Alexander from the corners of my eyes. He worked with energy, whistling as he did so. As he bent to his work, his wet breeches clung to his legs and bottom like a second skin. I smiled, averted my gaze and, guiltily, looked back again. I felt the colour rush to my face, wondering what Catherine would say.

I had no idea that Alexander was so skilled. He collected a pile of dry straw, took his pistol from his saddle, emptied the powder and scraped a spark from a tinderbox. When the powder ignited with a loud whoosh, the straw was instantly alight.

'That was clever,' I edged closer to the flames. Although gathering combustible materials had warmed me up slightly, I was still shivering.

'We'd better get out of these wet things,' Alexander said. 'It's not healthy.'

I stared at him. 'We can't sit here without clothes on!' The prospect both appalled and, strangely, beguiled me. I pushed away the thoughts that came to my mind. I might recall them later when I was alone.

'Look,' Alexander stepped away for a moment, returning with heavy woollen blankets folded over his arm. 'Horse blankets. They are not the most comfortable things to wear, but they'll cover us and they'll be warmer than what we have.'

He was right. 'Where can I change?' I peered into the gloom.

'You change beside the fire,' Alexander said. 'I'll go over there.' He indicated a dark corner. He touched my shoulder. 'It's all right, Mary. I won't look.'

'I know,' I said. I watched as Alexander lifted one of the blankets and walked into the dark. Turning my back, I struggled to remove my wet clothes. Hooks, eyes and buttons can be awkward, especially when dampness has swollen the material. Twice I turned abruptly to check that Alexander was not looking. He was as good as his word. The first time I saw him removing his waistcoat. The second time I had a flash of white flesh and looked away quickly, only to again turn back in guilty inquisitiveness. Although I just had a back view, I saw that Alexander was slim and muscular. I lingered for a few seconds before my conscience propelled me to concentrate on my undressing. The Elysian image remained with me.

'Are you ready?' Alexander's voice floated from the corner of the stable. 'May I come over?'

'Nearly ready.' Dragging off the last of my underclothes, I stood there with the fire roasting my front half and a draught chilling my back half. I had a most mischievous urge to call on Alexander now and allow him to see me in all my glory. I shook my head. It would be grossly unfair to embarrass the man in that manner. However, the tingle remained for a moment as I hauled on the horse blanket.

'I'm ready,' I said.

'Good,' Alexander walked over with his blanket like a rough coat. Piling his clothes on one of the bales of hay, he grinned to me. 'Well now, Mary. Isn't this an adventure to tell your grandchildren?'

'Yes indeed.' It was easy to smile to Alexander, even when wearing nothing but a blanket that itched most abominably. 'We'd better spread our clothes out in front of the fire.'

'Indeed, yes,' Alexander mirrored my words. 'I'll fetch some more wood.'

I watched as he moved to one of the stalls and destroyed it, hauling at the wood until the nails parted. He carried over lengths of timber and piled them beside the fire. 'Lady Emily won't like us breaking up her happy home.'

'Lady Emily can whistle.' I said.

The fire dispersed light as well as welcome warmth around the stable. That gloomy place became quite homely as we spread out our clothes beside the flames. I had no concern that the sight of my underthings should inflame Alexander. He seemed too well balanced a man for such nonsense. I felt entirely secure in his presence as if I had known him for years.

'There we are then.' Alexander said. 'All cosy and warm.' He scratched at his shoulder. 'These blankets are damnably uncomfortable though.'

'Damnably,' I said solemnly, and we laughed together.

'That rain seems as if it's on for the night,' Alexander said.

'I think so.' I said. I did not mind. I did not care one fig if it rained all night, all the next day and all the night after that. At that moment I was quite content to sit there beside that cheerful fire with a man who was not concerned that I wore a horse blanket for clothing while my hair was a shocking tangle, plastered to my head and dripping water down the back of my neck.

'Are you hungry?' Alexander broke what had been a surprisingly comfortable silence.

'I had not thought about it.' I said. 'Now you mention it, perhaps a little.'

'I'll see what I can find.' Alexander said. 'You wait here.'

'No, Alex.' Using the familiar diminutive, I shouted after him. 'Don't go out into the rain. I'm all right.' I may as well have tried to stop the tide. With his horse-blanket held around him like an opera cloak, Alexander padded bare-foot into the storm.

I sighed, watching the play of flames around the wood and listened to the batter of rain on the roof. Alexander was back within half an hour, water dripping from him but his arms full.

'Here we are,' he said. 'Nothing exotic.' He laid his treasures before him. 'We have two leaves full of bramble berries; the last of the crop so past their best but they will provide sweetness. We have half a basket of apples from Lady Emily's orchard. We have two trout from the burn, and half a dozen potatoes gleaned from the fields.'

'How did you catch the fish?' I looked at these various foodstuffs with some amazement. 'You've no rod or line.'

'I guddled them,' Alexander said. 'I had to discard the blanket first.'

'You guddled them? In the pouring rain?'

'Fish rise in the rain.' Alexander said.

I had a delightful vision of Alexander, naked as the day he was born, lying in the mud beside a frothing dark river, waiting with his hands in the water for a fish to swim close. That is the art of guddling, you see, catching the fish by hand and lifting it from the river. 'I'd like to have seen that,' I said with a wicked smile.

Alexander shook his head, smiling. 'It would not be the most attractive sight in the world.'

I thought of the brief view I had enjoyed of Alexander's nether regions. 'I'm not sure about that,' I said, and rapidly changed the subject. 'You'll be soaking.'

'I'll soon dry.' He pulled his blanket closer.

For one moment I contemplated offering to towel him dry. The thought was disturbingly delectable. I shook my head. *Don't be ridiculous. This man is Alexander, the eccentric plant collector.*

'Now,' Alexander lifted the trout. 'I have a knife in my jacket pocket,' he said. 'If you could pass it over, I'd be much obliged.'

As I pulled out the clasp-knife, Alexander's pocket-book fell out, to land on the ground at my feet. I handed over the knife and lifted the pocket-book. It had opened as it fell, with half the contents spilling out. I scooped up sundry silver and gold coins and a folded piece of parchment. About to replace it, I saw Alexander's look of agitation.

'I forgot that was there.' Alexander had left the circle of light from the fire to split and prepare the fish.

'What is it? May I look and see?'

'It's not worth it,' Alexander sounded more agitated than I had ever known him. 'It isn't worth it.'

Curious to find out what disturbed this most placid of men, I opened the paper. Inside, faded and pressed but still recognisable, was a single pink rose. I gave a subdued gasp. That was the dog rose I had presented to Alexander at Garleton Castle. I thought he would have laughed and thrown it away. Instead, he had preserved it within his pocketbook.

Why?

I could not ask him.

'I'll just put it back then.' Carefully refolding the rose within its paper, I replaced it in Alexander's pocketbook. That little rose must have meant a lot to Alexander for him to preserve it as he had. *Why? It was only a wild flower.* I looked up as Alexander returned. 'You are a strange man, Alexander,' I said.

'I've been called worse than that.' Alexander poked about on the wall of the stable. Finding what he sought, he returned with a large flat stone. 'Here's our griddle,' he said. 'It won't be the best cooking you'll have tasted.'

'I am sure it will be sublime.' I watched as Alexander built the fire up further, placed the flat stone on top and the cleaned fish on top of the stone. 'Don't burn yourself, now!'

'Too late,' Alexander said and sucked at his wrist.

'Oh, you silly boy! Let me see.' I held his hand, studying the angry red burn. 'Stay still.' Purely by instinct, I bent my head and kissed the burn. 'Is that better?'

Alexander stared at me as if I had sprouted wings. 'Yes.' His voice was small. 'Thank you.'

'It was only a healing kiss,' I withdrew rapidly.

Alexander stared at his wrist. 'I've only ever been kissed once before.'

'Only once?'

'When you kissed my forehead.' He touched the spot as if it was something sacred.

I tried to make a joke out of it. 'Surely your mother kissed you?'

'She was not an affectionate woman.'

'I see.' I said no more. What could I say? My mother was the opposite. She had hot emotions and showed them vividly. When I was younger and had earned praise, I got it in spades, together with kisses fit to drown a whale and hugs that would scare the most hugging of brown bears. I resolved, there and then, that I would never deprive any child of mine of kisses or affection. It was a good resolution.

I do not know what sort of oil Alexander used on the trout if indeed he used oil at all. I do know that they tasted as delicious as any fish that Cook ever produced, if a little smoky. Perhaps it was the novelty of the surroundings that enhanced the taste, or maybe it was the laughing company. I only know that I enjoyed every last morsel of that soft white flesh, with Alexander sitting opposite me in his blanket and the steam slowly coiling from our clothes.

'What's next?' I licked the grease from my fingers without a trace of embarrassment. 'You produced fish out of nowhere. What miracle are you going to do now?'

I had not seen Alexander push the potatoes into the base of the fire. Now he produced them.

'Here we are. I've no salt, I'm afraid.'

I looked at the blackened and charred lumps. 'We can't eat them,' I laughed.

'Watch.' Lifting the first potato, Alexander placed it on his knee and carefully cut away the blackened skin. He handed the white and tender interior to me. 'Try that.'

I did. 'It's edible,' I said with some surprise. 'No, it's even quite tasty.' It was good to see his smile of relief.

We ate side by side, saying little. I was as relaxed as I ever had been outside Cauldneb. 'I wonder what you're going to make next,' I said.

'Apple and bramble mush,' Alexander said. Once again he called his knife into use, peeling the apples, cutting them into small pieces and piling them, together with the bramble berries, onto the famous flat stone. I watched as he pounded them together and mixed them up. Balancing the mess on top of the fire for a few moments, Alexander lifted it down. He blew on his fingers as he placed the stone-plate between us.

'We eat with our fingers,' Alexander said solemnly. 'Dive in.'

I dived in. Looking back, we must have made a surreal picture, a young woman and a young man, dressed in nothing but horse-blankets, sitting around a fire in a draughty stable eating a makeshift meal with our fingers. It was a meal that I will never forget. That was the strangest time I had ever spent with a man. I compared it to Captain Ferintosh's sumptuous feast. There was no comparison. I had enjoyed Alexander's simple, experimental fare better. I still recall those few happy hours with a wistful smile. For a short time, fate had lifted the shadow of John Aitken. That shadow would soon return.

It was my destiny to wear the wedding ring of John Aitken. The darkness awaited beyond the stable doors. One cannot escape predetermination with a simple fire and a shared smile. Fate must have its way.

'That rain's getting heavier,' I said as the wind threatened to blow the roof from the stable.

'So it is.' Alexander did not seem concerned. 'We'd better stay here a little longer then.'

'Maybe we had,' I agreed without a qualm.

It was strange that I was quite content to sit quietly with Alexander. There was no need for conversation. When he spoke, I was equally happy to listen.

'I have never spent so long with a girl,' Alexander said.

'What do you normally do?' I avoided the *girl* subject. 'Hunt for plants?'

'Yes.' Alexander said. 'I gather plants, then identify and catalogue them, hoping to find a new variety.'

'Are the plants not pretty well known?' I was genuinely interested. 'I like gardening, particularly vegetables and fruit. Our gardener tries to teach me about varieties and such like things. I thought he knew them all.'

'Our Scottish plants are probably all well known,' Alexander's eyes lit up at this rare opportunity to discuss a subject close to his heart. 'I like to search for stranger plants, flowers, and what we call weeds that have come here from overseas. The more trade we have, the more likelihood there is of non-native plants arriving on our shores, maybe falling off a sack from Hindustan, or attached to a log from North America.'

I smiled at his enthusiasm. 'Wouldn't you like to go to Hindustan or Africa or some other foreign part to see what they have there?'

'I already have,' Alexander said.

'Have you?' I had not expected that reply.

'I spent two years in the Americas,' Alexander said. 'While the wealthy were off on the Grand Tour, I took ship for New York. I wandered the forests and mountains there.'

'When was that?' I had no idea that Alexander had travelled.

'1782 until 1784,' Alexander said.

'There was a war on then,' I pointed out.

'Yes,' Alexander agreed.

'You were fortunate not to get involved,' I said. I could not see Alexander carrying a sword and leading men into battle.

Alexander stared into the fire. 'There were a few occasions when I met the armies,' he said. 'I mainly managed to avoid them.' He looked up. 'That land is vast, Mary, much vaster than you can ever imagine. There is so much there, so much potential. I don't understand why men kill and maim for political ends when there is room and resources for us all.'

I looked at him. I had been a teenager when the last war had ended back in 1783. Since then there had been rumours of a new war with France. Half the young men in East Lothian had rushed to don scarlet uniforms and had strutted around like peacocks, boasting of the great deeds they would do. As far as I could see, all their great deeds would mean killing other young men exactly like themselves, except their uniform was a different colour and they spoke a foreign tongue. I had not been impressed. Alexander was the first young man I had ever met who did not either bore me or try to awe me with boasts of martial glory.

'There is nothing glorious in killing people,' Alexander could have read my thoughts.

'I agree,' I said. 'There is nothing glorious at all.'

We were silent for a few moments as the wind continued to howl around the eaves.

'My mother showed me how some plants could cure diseases.' Alexander looked hesitant as if he expected me to scoff at him. When I merely nodded, he continued. 'I would like to expand on that. I want to find plants to cure other illnesses.' He looked directly into my eyes. 'Could you imagine how much good that would do, Mary? Decades ago, James Lind from Edinburgh discovered that lime juice and fresh vegetables help cure scurvy, although the Navy has done nothing about it, so we lose thousands of seamen every year.'

'I did not know that,' I said.

'Could you imagine what treasures are out there, waiting for somebody to discover them?' I had never seen Alexander so enthusiastic about his plants; I had never seen any man so imbued with the desire to help humanity. This excitement was a new side to my eccentric companion.

'It is something I had not thought about,' I said.

'Think what good the potato has done since the Spanish brought it back from the Americas,' Alexander was in danger of falling into the fire in his enthusiasm. Even more interesting was that Alexander forgot he was wearing a loose blanket, which opened up when he gestured with his hands. I will leave the sights to your imagination. I can still smile at that captivating memory.

'Imagine what other sources of food are waiting for us to find them. We might discover the cure for any disease; measles, diphtheria, consumption, any of the fevers. We might find a cheap foodstuff that can end hunger or even famine forever!'

I hardly listened to Alexander's words. I was more impressed by his enthusiasm and desire to help. Speaking about varieties of plant, I had found a an entirely new variety of man; one I had never met before.

'How will you do all that, Alex?'

'I'll search the world,' Alexander said. 'I'll search the corners of the world that have never seen searched before. Europe is too small, too crowded, too well known. I want to look in the Americas, in Africa, in this Terra Australis that Captain Cook mapped for us all.'

I imagined Alexander scouring the highways and byways of the world for his plants. 'What a noble man you are,' I said. 'What a noble, inspiring, Christian project.'

'Every so often,' Alexander said. 'I will come home to catalogue what I have discovered. I will test the properties of each plant, each vegetable and each fruit.'

'You have your life mapped out, I see.'

Alexander nodded. 'I've never told anybody any of that before.' His enthusiasm faded. 'I don't know why I told you.'

I think I knew. I could not articulate my knowledge.

'You must consider me crazy.' Alexander's smile lacked its usual confidence. There was a sudden hesitation in the twist of his mouth. 'When I spoke about plants at school, the boys mocked me. So did the teachers, when they listened.'

'No,' I said. 'I don't think you are crazy.' I did not know what I thought. I could not even analyse my feelings. Or rather, I think I did know what I thought. I did not wish to admit it.

'It is as well that Mother put that barrier to prevent me finding a wife,' Alexander said. 'No woman would want a man to wander all over the world, leaving her at home.'

'No,' I agreed. 'No woman would want that.' I took a deep breath. 'Alexander,' I said, 'do you remember when we were in Wallace's Cave and you helped me put a note beside Captain Ferintosh's horses?'

'We did that well, didn't we?'

'We did,' I agreed. 'That was not what I was going to ask.' Now that I had started, I was not sure how to continue. Men were different, even painful, to talk to about emotional matters.

'What were you going to ask?' Alexander leaned forward, his eyes as intense as I had ever seen them.

'I am going to ask how you felt when you helped me with that note.' That was blunt even for me. I did not expect Alexander to tell me anything. All the men I knew would have avoided the question by giving a whimsical reply.

'I felt as if I was betraying you,' Alexander gave a direct answer without a trace of a smile.

'Why?' I pushed for more details.

'I knew Ferintosh was not right for you.' Alexander said. 'I like you too much to see a man hurt you.'

The words twisted in my insides. I had to push further, damn me for a fool. 'If you like me, then why did you not try to prevent the meeting?'

'I had no right to do such a thing,' Alexander said. 'I had no right to influence your life.' He was silent for quite a while. 'I had no right to prevent you from searching for happiness.'

'Even although it hurt you?' I was not sure for what I was looking.

'Even then.'

I nodded. 'You are a good friend, Alexander. A strange man, but a good friend.'

'The rain is easing.' Reaching over, Alexander fingered my dress, spread out on a bale of hay beside the fire. 'Your clothes are dry. I think we can dress and get you back home.'

Alexander was right. It was time to go. My mind was too full of words and images to add any more. I needed time alone to think.

I looked back inside the stables before we left. I was not sure what had happened in this dark, smoky place. I did know that I would never forget these few happy hours, perhaps my last carefree memories before my mother condemned me into marriage with a man far my senior.

Chapter Sixteen

For all the excitements of the past couple of weeks, one thing had dominated most of my thoughts. From the moment that my mother had mentioned her intention to marry me off to John Aitken, I had worried about the evening she intended to formalise our agreement. My passing, stupid infatuation with Captain Ferintosh had been a reaction to mother's statement. After all, Ferintosh was a rogue. I had known that I think, from the first or second time I had met him. In saying that, I missed him. Despite everything, I do not now regret the time I spent with that handsome, wicked man.

Saturday evening. I felt sick. I had grown to quite like Mr Aitken, for all his advanced years and physical weaknesses. He was, as Mrs Mackay had said, a kindly man. But I did not love him. I could not love him. I could not ever see myself as marrying him. The thought of kissing him, let alone having other more personal intimacy, repulsed me.

As the hour of Mr Aitken's arrival drew close, I contemplated my options. I could stay and brazen it out, giving a firm *no* to my mother's hopes. I did not know how she would react. I did not even know if my decision would be legal. My second option was to smile nicely and agree to the wedding. My mother would be pleased and, judging from what I had seen; Mr Aitken would be an amiable enough husband, with bouts of grouchiness expected in an old man. I thought of the third option: run.

I had considered that choice already. Now I examined it in increasing desperation. I could pack up what I could, grab Coffee and head for ... Head for where? I had nowhere to go. I could perhaps ride to Edinburgh and find a job as a governess if I were extremely fortunate. I would be little more than a paid servant, a teacher of other people's children. I could have wept with frustration. If there was somebody I knew well, somebody to give me sanctuary, somebody that knew me better than they knew my parents, I could have, I would have, run there. There was nobody.

I knew dozens of people. I was acquainted with all the local farmers and their families, all the minor gentry of East Lothian, but so were father and mother. None of them would hide me. I thought of Catherine Brown, my most particular friend. Would he help? Yes, she would if I asked. Could she help? No; her father was as close a friend of father's as I was of Catherine's.

'Mother,' I nearly pleaded. 'Do you have to invite Mr John Aitken?'

'Yes, I do,' Mother said. 'You know that you and he are getting quite friendly now.'

'I do not wish to marry him.'

'You will wish to marry him,' Mother said. 'I know you better than you know yourself.'

I spent much of Saturday afternoon lying in my bed, fighting my fears and trying to work out how to escape. I could not think of a way. I considered fleeing to Alexander Colligere and pleading for sanctuary, until I realised that I did not know where he lived. That was strange; I knew every other man and woman by their houses or farms. Despite having met Alexander Colligere a few times, I did not know much about him. He merely appeared and disappeared, seemingly at will. Like a fairy, or his witch of a mother.

I was alone.

That thought, for a young woman on the cusp of official adulthood, was sobering. It made me think of my position in the world, both now and in the future. A woman without a fortune of her own needed a husband. I had the usual female accomplishments, but I could do no useful work except the lowest and least paid. Reality bit hard. Now, you may have read all Sir Walter Scott's novels, in which case you will believe that Scots are all romantic dreamers who wish for the return of some mythical Stuart king. The reality is somewhat different. The average Scot is the most hard-headed pragmatist known to humanity. We are about as romantic as a midden heap. Our history has made us a race of survivors, and that includes matters of romance or lack of it.

The debacle with Captain Ferintosh had somewhat dented my childish belief in romance. No chivalric knights were riding to rescue damsels in distress; there were few marriages of never-ending bliss. Now I sought something more permanent than a fleeting kiss, charming manners and fine clothes. I had learned that it was what a man was like inside that mattered.

I now knew that inside his somewhat unprepossessing exterior, John Aitken was a good man. He would not beat me, as I had heard happened in some marriages. He would not deny me affection; when I visited him in Tyneford he had been the most pleasant of companions. His house was well run and comfortable. I could be happy there. All I lacked was love. Many marriages managed to survive without that single ingredient. No, I told myself severely, John Aitken is a good man.

Armed with that nugget of information, I asked Mother if I could have a bath before John Aitken arrived.

'I would like to look my best,' I glanced down at myself. 'The last couple of weeks have been difficult. I am bruised and weather-battered, with the smell of smoke in my hair.'

Mother's pleasure could not have been more evident. 'What an excellent idea!'

I was a little guilty at giving the maids extra work, so I helped them carry the bath to the front of the fire in my room. I even carried up some of the pails of hot water myself, slopping it over the floor as I did so. Eventually, it was all set up. I stripped to the skin and stepped in, allowing the gentle warmth to seep into my body. Baths were not as frequent in my youth as they are now, so young Maggie hovered to see this novelty, pretending to wish to help me.

'Are you bathing to get ready for Mr Aitken's visit, Miss Mary?'
Honestly, Mother was right. I allowed far too much familiarity from
the servants. I ignored her question. 'Have you ever had a bath, Maggie?'

'Why, no Miss.' Maggie widened her eyes and giggled at the idea.

'You should try it sometime,' I said. 'It's very relaxing.'

'What if a man walked in when you were all naked, Miss?'

I smiled. 'A gentleman would knock at the door, first.'

'What if they didn't knock first?' Maggie said. 'What if Mr Hepburn
was to walk in by mistake, or one of the footmen.' She looked down
at me, giggling. 'Or even Mr Aitken.'

'Oh, Lord, no!' I had nearly reconciled myself to the thought of John
Aitken as a husband, yet Maggie's words shocked me. The thought of
that balding old man finding me like this! I shook my head. 'I hope it
never happens, Maggie.'

'Or one of the younger gentlemen, Miss,' Maggie was too young to
know when she had said enough. 'Mr Ormiston maybe, or that strange
man with the kind eyes.'

'That strange man with the kind eyes? Who do you mean, Maggie?'

'That tall fellow that sometimes walks around the grounds, Miss. I
saw him fall into the haha a few days ago.'

We had a haha, a sunken barrier with a turfed incline, around our
immediate gardens to prevent the livestock straying where they could
do damage. I was not aware of anybody having fallen down the slope.

'I don't know of any tall fellow with kind eyes.' My first thought was
of Captain Ferintosh, but he was safely incarcerated in Haddington, if
not in Edinburgh by now.

'He was there again this morning, Miss.' Maggie said. 'I wonder if
he is still there.' She tripped to the window, stifling her giggle.

I lay back, luxuriating in the bath as I lazily soaped myself. I hoped
that Mr Aitken did not turn up. *No*, I thought, *he will turn up. He is one
of those solid, reliable men, the sort one wishes for a husband.* I sighed.
*Mother had chosen well. Except for his age and appearance, Mr Aitken
had all the attributes of a good husband, damn him.*

'I can see him!' Maggie trilled. 'What is that man doing?'

'Who? Mr Aitken?' I looked up, not wishing to leave my warm bath on a whim.

'No,' Maggie shook her head. 'That strange man. He is climbing a tree!'

'Who is climbing a tree?' Sighing, I climbed out of the bath, allowing a cascade of water to slop on the floor, and sloshed wetly to the window. Edging Maggie aside, I peered through the glass. 'Where?'

'There, Miss,' Maggie pointed to an elm tree that spread its branches to within a few feet of the house. 'Just there.'

I had been looking too far away. I adjusted my view and started. Alexander, possibly attracted by the flurry of movement, stared straight at me. 'Oh!' I covered my mouth. I stood still, unable to move as Alexander and I perused each other from a distance of two yards.

If I was astonished, Alexander was more so. He was fully clothed; I was fully naked.

'Oh, Lord!' Turning, I ran back to the bath and immersed myself in the soapy water. 'Oh, Lord! Oh, Lord!' I sunk right down as if to hide from Alexander's view. 'Oh, Lord!'

'Oh, Miss,' Maggie was still at the window. 'He's fallen down! He's fallen from the tree!'

'Oh, Lord,' I said for about the fifth or was it the sixth time? 'Has he hurt himself?' I left the bath again, suddenly concerned.

'No, Miss. He's on his feet.'

Feeling a little foolish, I returned to the bath, which had lost much of its appeal with all the to-ing and fro-ing.

'He's walking away, Miss,' Maggie said.

'As long as he's not hurt.'

'Is he a Peeping Tom, Miss?' Maggie perched herself, uninvited, on my dressing table. Clearly, she had not yet learned the decorum necessary for all good servants. 'Shall I call for the footman to throw him out of the grounds?' She wriggled her bottom to get more comfortable, knocking down two of my precious bottles of scent.

'No,' I shook my head. 'That is Mr Alexander Colligere. He is the least likely man in the world to be a Peeping Tom. He was probably searching for some new form of plant. Was he looking into my window?'

'No, Miss,' Maggie shook her head quite firmly. 'Not unless he has eyes in his doup.'

I shook my head. These young girls had no idea of decorum or respectable language. I tried not to smile. 'He was not facing this way, then.'

'No, Miss. He was bending over the branch looking at something.'

'He could not have been a Peeping Tom then,' I said.

'No, Miss. But when you came to the window, he saw you.'

I nodded. Poor Alexander must have got quite a fright, looking for a plant or an insect or a piece of lichen, only to find a naked me staring at him. I could not prevent my smile. 'He must have been surprised.'

'Yes, Miss,' Maggie's giggle proved so infectious that in a second we were both laughing. 'What would you do if he came in here to apologise, Miss?'

I imagined the scene. Alexander was so unconventional that he might do such a thing. I thought of him walking in, open-handed and open-eyed, ready to apologise. I smiled again. 'I would stand up and accept his apology,' I said, imagining the sight, imagining Alexander's reaction.

'Yes, Miss,' Maggie said. 'The poor fellow would likely faint on the spot!'

'Then I would have to revive him,' I said. 'With a strong dose of smelling salts and a kiss on the lips!'

'Oh, Miss!' Maggie was giggling so much she could hardly speak. 'You are terrible!'

For a moment we were not mistress and servant but two young women sharing an amusement. We laughed for a few moments until I tried to control myself. 'I heard a story once,' I spoke as gravely as I could. 'There was a gentleman who walked into a lady's boudoir by mistake when she was taking a bath,' I indicated myself in case Maggie had forgotten what I was doing. 'The gentleman bowed and said, "My apologies, sir." I don't know if I would be relieved or insulted if a man said that to me.'

Maggie shook her head. 'He must be a very short-sighted gentleman not to notice the difference between a man and a woman, Miss. In your case, it is very evident.'

I was not prepared to discuss such details with anybody except Catherine Brown. 'I heard of another instance,' I said slowly, 'where the gentleman concerned felt obliged to propose marriage to the lady.'

'Oh Miss!' Maggie laughed again. 'What if that strange tree-climbing gentleman did happen to walk in?'

I did not laugh. I looked at the door, wondering what I would do if Alexander opened it and walked in while I was in the bath. The thought was quite disturbing, in an altogether interesting way.

Alexander: that strange, homely, comfortable man. I closed my eyes, allowing my thoughts to wander where they would, exploring avenues I had never before considered.

'Miss?' Maggie was kneeling at my side. 'The water's getting cold miss. You'll catch a chill if you're not careful.'

'Yes, thank you, Maggie.' My thoughts had taken me away from reality, losing my sense of time and place.

I had resigned myself to meeting John Aitken. The brief encounter with Alexander, coupled with my day-dreams, had unsettled me again, so I was in a bad fettle when poor Maggie helped me dress. I snarled at her when she fumbled my buttons, glowered when she hooked the eyes in the wrong sequence and threatened to slap her when she stepped on the hem of my dress.

'I'm sorry Miss.' Poor Maggie was nearly in tears, after having been so friendly with me only a few moments before.

'So am I,' I said, recovering my temper. I have said that I was bad tempered; I was also quick to restore my normal disposition. I did not like to upset anybody, particularly a servant who could not retaliate. 'I did not mean that Maggie, I should not have said it and I would never slap you. I do apologise. You have done nothing wrong.'

'It's all right, Miss,' Maggie was one of these sunny, cheerful girls who are a delight to know.

All the same, my mood remained foul when I eventually clumped down the stairs in my clumsy best shoes, with my wide dress rustling against the bannisters and my hair piled up so high that I had to duck to get under the door frame. The things we do in the name of fashion. Sometimes I could wish we were all like the Hottentots or Cherokees or such like and could wear the minimum of clothing without any fuss. Still, I suppose that our weather forbids such extremes of *au naturel*. As it was, my mother inspected me minutely, making unnecessary adjustments to my dress before finally nodding her satisfaction.

'You'll do, I suppose' Mother said, which was probably as high praise as any Scottish matron can rise to when formally introducing her daughter to her prospective husband.

I was unused to formal meals in Cauldneb. We usually sat all together like pigs at a trough, with the servants walking in and out whenever they pleased, making comments on the conversation and generally acting like members of the family. That evening I sat in rigid uncomfortableness if there is such a word, stiff-backed and grumpy while we awaited our guest of honour.

Although I had been expecting it, I still started at the sound of the door. I half rose from my chair.

'Sit there,' Mother ordered curtly. 'I don't wish you to move until Mr Aitken appears through that door. Then you rise and greet him like a lady.'

'I've met him often,' I complained, for the whalebone corset was crushing my ribs so I could hardly breathe, while my shoes were pinching my poor toes. 'There is no need for this unaccountable formality.'

'There is every need!' Mother's snapping tone proved that her nerves were also jangling. 'We have to show that we are as capable of respectability as any other family in the neighbourhood. Mr Aitken has seen you on horseback and grubbing about in the mud. It's high time he saw you at your best.'

I could not think of a time that Mr Aitken had seen me grubbing about in the mud as Mother so elegantly put it. However, this did not seem like the best time to question her. In a contest of hotness of temper, she had better than twenty years advantage over me.

'Wait here,' Mother instructed coldly.

I waited, staring at the table with its array of our best china set on a crisp linen table-cloth. I heard the rumble of voices from the withdrawing room next door; I heard mother's light tones welcoming the guest, or guests to judge by the number of voices, and father's gruffness joining in. There was the pleasant tinkle of glasses as everybody fortified themselves for the ordeal of a formal dinner. Everybody except me, I noted, left alone to stagnate.

'Mary!' Mother opened the door to warn me my destiny was imminent.

I stood up with my heart pounding. The moment I had dreaded was closing in on me. This coming hour or two might close the arrangement for my marriage. Before this night ended, I would in all probability be engaged to marry a much older man. I took a deep breath, wondering again if I could simply refuse.

I could. I told myself. I must. I did not wish to condemn myself to a misalliance with a greybeard. . It would be bad enough now, with Mr Aitken in his forties. In ten years time, he would be approaching sixty, a man in his dotage, and I would be scarcely thirty, a woman in my prime. I shuddered at the prospect. I could not go through with it. I would not go through with it.

Somebody pushed the door further open. The rumble of voices increased. The housekeeper and footmen entered, dressed in their most formal attire. They did not smile as they took up positions against the wall. Mother was next to enter, walking stiffly to her seat. She stood beside it, motioning for me to stand. I obeyed, feeling sick.

Mr John Aitken entered next, beautifully dressed. I tried not to notice that his waistcoat strained to hold back his expanding stomach. He bowed to me.

'Miss Hepburn.'

'Mr Aitken,' I dropped in a curtsey as if I had never met the man before.

I was surprised when Alexander was next to enter. Although he was dressed as formally as Mr Aitken, he did not bow. 'Halloa, Mary,' he said, grinning.

'Mr Colligere.' With mother present, I had to ignore his welcome friendliness and drop into a curtsey. As I rose, I remembered his face staring through the window at my unclothed person only a couple of hours earlier. My face was flaming red, much to Mother's amusement. She said nothing, but I read the laughter in her eyes, amidst irritation I did not understand.

'You two are already very informal,' Mother said as Father took his place at the head of the table.

'Mr Colligere and I are already acquainted,' I said.

'Mr Colligere?' Mother looked puzzled. 'Pray, who is Mr Colligere?'

'It's the name my friends call me,' Alexander said artfully. 'I've been called that ever since I was at school.'

I managed to control my surprise. 'Is it not your name, sir?' I felt my face burning again. I had managed to call Alexander by the wrong name at a formal gathering, as well as on every occasion we had met.

'Good Lord, no, Mary!' Alexander shook his head so that his queue must have clattered against his ears. 'It is a nickname. It is a joke, a Latin tag that means *to gather together.*' He smiled. 'It is a pun on my hobby, you see; even as a youngster I was collecting and gathering specimens of plant life. I got myself into all sorts of bother over it.' He grinned again.

'I apologise for any offence I have caused, sir,' I felt about an inch tall. 'I did not know.'

'Offence? What offence could you ever cause me, Mary?' Alexander looked surprised at the idea. 'You are the least offensive girl in the world!'

Mother spoke then, tactfully turning the conversation away from the subject of my inoffensiveness. 'Have you found anything of interest in your searches?'

'My word, yes,' Alexander's eyes lit with delight at this opportunity to talk about his obsession. He launched into a list of plants, giving the names in both Scots and English before adding the Latin tag. 'And there are other benefits too,' he said after a lengthy discourse which I found quite interesting, despite Mother's glazed-eye look. 'Why, this very morning I was up a tree in Mr Hepburn's policies when, quite by chance, I came across the most splendid view.'

That little sally coloured me so hotly that I am surprised I did not set the wall-paper alight. I sensed Mother's gaze on me and clamped my mouth as tightly shut as the Royal Naval blockade of Brest.

'The most splendid view it is possible to imagine,' Alexander continued. 'It was something more delightful than any number of plants.'

I said nothing, wishing I could land a hefty slap on Alexander's animated face while I rushed out of the room to hide forever.

'Pray tell us, sir, what that view might have been?' Mother asked the question.

'I am sure there is no need,' I tried to stem the avalanche of my embarrassment.

'The view over the delights of Cauldneb was sublime,' Alexander spoke without a fragment of guilt.

'We have worked hard to make this estate the finest in the county,' Father's mind rarely strayed far from his policies, his fields and his livestock. I blessed his honest simplicity.

Mother looked slightly disappointed. I suspected that she knew more than she was saying. 'Here comes the soup,' she changed the conversation.

We dedicated the next few moments to Cook 's fish soup. I had half expected Mr Aitken to creak down on one aged knee and pose the question the moment he entered the room, so was grateful for every minute of freedom. All the same, it was the most exquisite torture to sit at that table pretending to enjoy the meal while waiting for my world to collapse.

'Well now,' Mother said as we sat in silence. 'This is a pleasant gathering.'

'Yes, indeed,' Mr Aitken said. 'It was very kind of you to invite us round.'

'You have been more than helpful to Andrew with this Edmund Charleton affair,' Mother said.

'It was my duty,' Mr Aitken said.

'You and your son put yourselves at risk,' Mother continued. 'Andrew and I are most grateful to you, Mr Aitken.' Her tone hardened so slightly that only Father and I would be able to recognise the alteration. 'Is that not so, Andrew?'

'Oh, very grateful,' Father said. 'John, that is, young John, John Alexander,' Father addressed Alexander, as he returned to the pre-soup conversation. 'What impressed you most about Cauldneb? I have been addressing the drainage of the top fields this past year; the water runs off the muir onto my fields, causing me all sorts of problems. I dug new drains to counteract the water.'

I missed the remainder of Father's conversation as I analysed his initial words. *Young John, John Alexander?* I waited for a gap in the conversation, which was a long time coming as the three gentlemen discussed the mechanics of field drainage, the best use of labour and the most efficient methods of using the resulting excess water.

'I was thinking of creating a reservoir,' Father was enthusiastic about his subject. Unable to wait any longer, I had to interrupt.

'Alexander,' I said. 'Is your given name John?'

'That's right,' Alexander said. 'Didn't you know that?'

'No,' I said. 'I thought you were Alexander Colligere, remember?' I reminded him of my stupidity.

'Oh, no. I am John Alexander Aitken. I use my middle name to avoid confusion with my father, John Aitken senior.'

'I believed there was only one Mr John Aitken,' I said.

I felt my mother's gaze on me again as my heartbeat increased until I thought it would take a life of its own and fly out of my poor beleaguered breast.

'Mary, dear,' that was a bad sign; Mother only called me dear at times of crisis. 'Could you please step outside the room for a moment?

I wish to speak to you.' Mother's charming smile fooled nobody as she excused herself. 'This is mother, daughter business,' she said. 'I'm sure you understand.'

'Of course,' Mr John Aitken waved a fork. 'Women's talk, eh? I do hope that Miss Hepburn is not in trouble.'

'So do I, sir, 'I forced a smile. My legs were shaking as I rose from the table.

Father gave me an encouraging wink while Alexander surreptitiously touched my hand as I passed him. That was all very friendly, perhaps, but less than helpful when I closed the door and Mother took me unceremoniously by the sleeve and dragged me into an unused guest bedroom.

'Alexander Colligere?' Mother pushed her face to within an inch of my nose.

'I thought that was his name,' I said.

Mother shook her head. 'That is John Aitken,' she had difficulty controlling her voice. 'That is the young fellow I have been mentioning for the past weeks.'

My heart was pounding like East Lothian surf in a north-easterly gale. 'Oh, dear Lord in heaven. Not Mr John Aitken, not his father.' I gasped out the words. 'I thought you meant...'

'You thought I meant to marry you off to a man old enough to be your father?' Mother looked incredulous. 'Good God, Mary! What sort of ogre do you think I am?'

I should have known better, I really should. I shook my head. 'I don't think you are any sort of ogre,' I said.

'I knew the moment I met him that you and young John, Alexander or whatever you wish to call the poor fellow, are well suited.'

I felt the breath catch in my throat. 'I love him.'

I had not meant to say that. The words came from nowhere. I had not even allowed myself to think them.

'I know.' Mother said. 'I knew you would.'

I stared at her. 'You knew? How? No,' I shook my head. 'It does not matter. What happens now?' I thought how comfortable I was with

Alexander, how easy it was to talk to him, how we laughed without restrictions and told each other our deepest secrets without fear. Oh, dear God, I did love him so.

'That is up to you and Jo- Alexander.' Mother straightened the collar of my gown. 'Look at you, like a sack of potatoes, no two pounds of you hanging straight. It's a wonder that John Alexander would even look at you let alone anything else.'

'He looked at me through the window,' I blurted out. 'When I was in the bath.'

'Good,' Mother was not as scandalised as I expected. 'That will raise his interest even further. Come on Mary; the men will be wondering what's happened to us.' She shook her head. 'Dear heavens woman, did you honestly believe I wanted you to marry John senior? I don't know,' she gave me a sharp slap on the rump, followed quickly by a hug. 'Go in, then, Mary!'

The last time I entered the dining room I had been in a state of acute depression, dreading a future married to an old man. This time I was elated, so excited that I could hardly feel the floor under my feet as I hoped to hear Alexander's declaration of love and proposal of marriage, which I fully intended to accept. However, fate has a way of keeping its cruellest cut to the last. Have you noticed how things are never as bad as you think they are going to be? Well, they are never as good either. There was another bitter twist to this tangled tale.

Mr Aitken looked up as we re-entered the room. 'Is everything all right?' He asked. 'I do hope that Miss Hepburn is not in any trouble.'

'Mary is not in any trouble with me,' Mother resumed her seat at the foot of the table.

'I am glad to hear it,' Mr Aitken said. 'When she arrived at Tyneford with her message a day or so ago, she looked worn out. I felt quite paternal toward her.'

Paternal. The word rattled around my head. That was the expression on Mr Aitken's face. That was why he was so gentle and kind to me. It was not love, or at least not the kind of love I had thought. It was the affection of a man to his daughter or daughter-in-law. That meant that Alexander must have been discussing me with his father. I looked at Alexander, wondering when he would make his declaration.

He was certainly in no rush. Alexander did not bring up the possibility of marriage during that meal, despite his father dropping broad hints.

'You have a fine daughter, Mr Hepburn,' Mr Aitken said. 'She will make somebody an excellent wife.'

'I believe she will,' Father spoke too loudly. He was never a man for subterfuge. 'I heard that there is a man from Musselburgh searching for a wife.'

That was the first blatant lie I had heard my father say.

'He'd better be quick then,' Mother joined in. 'Our Mary is a good catch.'

'Couldn't be better,' Mr Aitken said.

You can imagine how I felt. I sat on my hard chair, literally squirming in embarrassment as everybody sang my imaginary praises. Everybody, that was, except the only man whose opinion really mattered. Alexander sat there dumb until I felt like taking a long pin and sticking it hard into what Maggie would call his doup to make him wake up and propose to me. Oh, I would make him jump! That thought consoled me for a few moments without in the least advancing my position.

It was Mr Aitken; bless his balding head, who finally got Alexander to move. Unfortunately, Alexander's reaction was not what I wished.

'Well, John,' I was interested to hear that John Aitken called his son John. It must only be outsiders that called him Alexander. 'You've heard our conversation.'

'Yes, Father,' Alexander gave his characteristic grin.

'Do you have anything to say?' That was the most direct hint so far.

I saw Mother's face; she glanced at Father and then at me in high expectation.

'No, Father.'

These two words tumbled my dreams around me. I could have swept out of that room in a cascade of tears and anger. I did not.

When Mr Aitken looked at me, I could read the apology in his face. Well, I was not inclined to sit and wait on the shelf until spiders spun cobwebs around my head. Why should men always take the initiative?

I took a deep breath. 'Well, Alexander, you and I have got to know each other over the past few weeks.'

I could feel the tension in the atmosphere. Mother nodded encouragement.

'I know that you discussed me at Tyneford,' I put my cards on the table, one by one, aware that everyone in the room was listening. 'I do not know how much you like me.' I waited in vain for a response.

It was harder than I thought, proposing to a man in front of a critical audience. However, I had set my cap on it, and I am not a woman to easily give up. I took a deep breath.

'I love you, Alexander.'

There. That was it said. That was my queen of hearts out in the open with no secrets.

Alexander stared at me, with concern in his fate.

I played my ace.

'Will you marry me, John Alexander Aitken?'

I could not be any more direct than that.

Alexander responded with his joker.

'I can't.'

Oh, dear Lord. Oh dear Lord, no!

'Why the devil not?' John Aitken nearly shouted the words. 'By God, man, she's a peach! A veritable peach and she likes you, loves you, God knows why! You'll never get a better, by God!'

Alexander stood up so abruptly that he would have upset the table had it not been of the sturdiest Scottish oak. I remained still. I could feel my mother's anguish. I felt sick.

'I can't!' Alexander repeated.

I tried to catch his eye. I failed.

'Why can't you?' I spoke quietly, not far from tears.

In answer, Alexander reached inside his jacket and produced the folded, sealed piece of parchment he had shown me a few days ago and about which I had forgotten entirely. He dropped it on the table. 'That is why.'

'What the deuce?' John Aitken lifted it. 'It's tied and sealed.'

'Mother gave me that.' Alexander said. 'She wrote the name of my future wife on the paper.'

'Well?' John Aitken tossed the paper back to Alexander. 'Open the damned thing and read Mary's name.'

That is when I realised the true difficulty of Alexander's position. He had only one choice. If he opened the paper and the name was not the woman he chose, he would have thrown away his life. Holding Alexander's gaze, I lifted my eyebrows.

'I am not forcing you,' I said.

Alexander's sudden grin lit up the room. 'Oh, damn it all,' he said. 'I'm going to marry you whatever the paper says. It's my choice and nobody else's.' He looked at me with his grin widening. 'Except yours.'

I tilted my head to one side. 'I am not forcing you,' I repeated. 'You already know my thoughts. I defy any witch, East Lothian or other, to try to destroy my love for you.'

Although we all watched as Alexander untied the faded ribbon, broke the red seal and unfolded the paper, I doubt that the others in that room experienced the same heart-pounding tension as I did. My mouth was dry as a sawyer's yard in midsummer.

Alexander took one glance at the paper, read the name silently, folded it again and replaced it in his pocket. His smile had not faltered, but his face was ashen beneath the tan.

'Well?' I demanded.

'We'll make the arrangements as soon as we can,' Alexander said. 'There is no sense in waiting for these things.'

'The name,' I insisted. 'Was it Mary?'

'The name does not matter,' Alexander said. 'I love you, and you love me. That's all that matters.'

I could see the horror in his eyes. I knew he would marry me whatever price he had to pay. This strange plant hunter was my man. We belonged together. I was not prepared to marry him if it ruined his life.

'What name was written?' I kept my voice under control. 'What name was on the paper? If there is a better girl for you, Alexander, I swear by all that is holy that I shall spend the rest of my life helping you find her.'

I was not merely saying that. It was true. I loved this man. I had not realised that until this morning. I loved him so much that it hurt. I loved him so much that I was prepared to sacrifice my happiness to grant him his, as I knew he was ready to do the same for me. He had already proved that he would do the same for me, with Captain Ferintosh.

Alexander stood up. 'Mary Hepburn,' he said quietly. 'Will you do me the honour of becoming my wife?'

I wanted to say yes. I wanted desperately to throw myself at Alexander, hold him and keep holding him for the rest of my life. 'No.' Shaking my head, I stood up, knocking my chair onto the floor. 'No, Alexander. I will not. I will not put you through a life of misery.'

We stared at each other, two young people painfully in love with a barrier between us that neither of us wished or could understand. Two young people trapped by a woman who was long dead.

It was my mother who broke the terrible silence. 'Now listen to me, Mary! I've had just about enough of this nonsense. I don't believe in witchcraft or curses or any of that rubbish. You will accept this man's offer and take him as your husband! You hear me, Mary Agnes Hepburn? I will take on any pretended witch and challenge her false power! I will stand between you and any curse!'

That was my mother at her best.

Alexander blinked. I saw some of the colour return to his face. 'Mrs Hepburn,' he said. 'What did you call Mary?'

'I called her by her name: Mary Agnes Hepburn, and I say the same to you, John Alexander Aitken. You can forget all about witches. Love is more powerful than any such thing.'

'Yes, Mother,' Alexander slid his hand back inside his pocket. He produced the folded paper and placed it, oh-so-carefully, on to the table.

I ignored it. Mother was right. Our love was too strong for any curse to spoil.

'Let me see.' Father reached forward and opened the paper. There were only three letters on it. MAH.

M. A. H.

My initials: Mary Agnes Hepburn.

'Oh, dear God in his heaven,' Alexander said. 'Mary Agnes Hepburn. Now I will ask again. Will you marry me, Mary Agnes Hepburn?'

'Alexander,' I said softly. 'You told me, only a few days ago, that no women would wish a husband who wandered all over the world most of the time, leaving her at home.' I saw the sudden doubt shadow his eyes.

'I said that,' Alexander said.

I knew he was preparing himself for a disappointment. 'I would not like that either. I want to be with you when you wander all over the world. I want to be with you when you return to Cauldneb with our discoveries. I want to be with you every day wherever you are. In short, John Alexander Aitken, my answer is yes.'

I did not have the opportunity to say more as Alexander pressed his lips against mine for his third, and undoubtedly, his best yet, kiss.

So you see why I grew reconciled to my name. It is not a pretty name. It is not a distinguished name, but it is all my own. If I had been called anything else, I might not have had such a happy marriage to Alexander. Mary Agnes Hepburn, I was and Mary Agnes Hepburn I remain, although I can also use my married name of Mary Agnes Aitken if I so desire.

And that is my story, and here it ends.

Good night and joy be with you all.

Historical Notes

Illicit Distilling

In the late 18th and early 19th century, illicit distilling was a black industry throughout Scotland. It is nearly impossible to pick up a Scottish newspaper of the period without coming across some reference to a still being located, or a skirmish between the Excisemen and illegal distillers. Although most of these stills were small-scale affairs, others were of industrial size. Often large gangs of armed men escorted the whisky from the still in the deep countryside to the major population centres where the smugglers sold it.

Agricultural Revolution

The Industrial Revolution is well known. Most people will be aware that Scotland was at the forefront of the process of industrialisation, with many of the innovations of steam power and the associated machinery coming from this small nation. What is not so well known is that an agricultural revolution preceded the industrial advances. Again, Scotland was at the forefront, with improvements in agricultural machinery, drainage, methods of crop cultivation, enclosures and stock rearing. Without these improvements, it is unlikely that the growing population of Industrial Britain could have been fed.

Scottish Plant Hunters

In the Eighteenth and Nineteenth centuries, Scotland produced a plethora of explorers. Most were concerned with geographical discoveries, such as the source of the Nile, or the whereabouts of Timbuktu or the North Pole. Others were hoping to stop the slave trade in Africa, while a small and dedicated band were searching for new plants. These latter men worked for what is now the Royal Horticultural Society, the Botanical Gardens of Edinburgh or Glasgow or for wealthy patrons. The plants they introduced to this country, and to the world, have proved immense in increasing our scientific knowledge as well as enhancing gardens the length and breadth of the nation.

For instance, there was George Don (1764 – 1814) who travelled from the Gambia to the USA, David Douglas (1799 – 1834), after whom the Douglas Fir is named and Francis Masson (1741-1805) who sought plants in South Africa, the West Indies, USA and Canada.

John Alexander Aitken is, of course, fictitious, but as a representative of a dedicated group, I hope he had a productive and happy life with Mary Hepburn. I am sure he did have.

Helen Susan Swift
Haddington, Lammermuir, Garleton Hills and Aberdeen, November, 2018

Dear reader,

We hope you enjoyed reading *The Name of Love*. Please take a moment to leave a review, even if it's a short one. Your opinion is important to us.

Discover more books by Helen Susan Swift at
https://www.nextchapter.pub/authors/helen-susan-swift

Want to know when one of our books is free or discounted for Kindle? Join the newsletter at http://eepurl.com/bqqB3H

Best regards,

Helen Susan Swift and the Next Chapter Team

You might also like:

Storm of Love (Lowland Romance Book 5) by Helen Susan Swift

To read first chapter for free, head to:
https://www.nextchapter.pub/books/storm-of-love

Books by the Author

- The Handfasters (Lowland Romance Book 1)
- The Tweedie Passion (Lowland Romance Book 2)
- A Turn of Cards (Lowland Romance Book 3)
- The Name of Love (Lowland Romance Book 4)
- Dark Mountain
- Dark Voyage
- The Malvern Mystery
- Sarah's Story
- Women of Scotland

Made in the USA
Las Vegas, NV
29 October 2021

33252657R00114